ASCENDANT

THE MYSTICAL VEIL
BOOK 4

Shelley Dorey

Contents

THE STORY SO FAR

The Mystical Veil is a Four Book Series that concludes with this episode, Ascendant

Book 1: Legacy

At 23, Keira Swanson had a pretty sweet life. Born into wealth, she was free to try her hand at anything she wanted. Not that she worked very hard at it. For her, the important things in life revolved around the club scene in Manhattan.

In a New York minute this changed radically. Her parents finally drew a line after her last self inflicted failure and kicked her out. Not only did they cut off her too generous allowance, her only option was to live with a grandmother she never knew she had. In Canada of all places! Keira finds out the hard way that there's another Kingston besides the party central city in Jamaica.

Meeting Pamela York was life changing. Keira is introduced to the unseen world of the spirits of those who have died. These ghosts weren't just haunting certain places, their very presence alongside the living created disruption in the universe. It had been Pamela's life work to convince these lost souls to pass through The Mystical Veil and maintain the harmony of the cosmos.

Ready or not, Keira takes on Pamela's work in a heartfelt passing of the torch.

Book 2: Heritage

Keira's not alone in her work. Just as Pamela had someone to look out for her, Keira's developed a close friendship with a quirky letter carrier. There aren't many postal workers who are also highly trained in Physics.

Physics? Not Psychic? Nope; Physics. Einstein, Stephen Hawking, e=mc2 kind of stuff. Math. LOTS of math. Ewww... But Gwen's awesome. A lanky redhead, she looks after her father Devon. He's a widower suffering from MS. Together, Keira and Gwen travel the world guiding the forlorn dead to their destiny.

After a spat, Gwen vanishes. To make matters worse Keira is stunned to learn she has dangerous enemies. People who want to use her abilities; not for harmony, but in a lust for power. David Holmes is such a man. Driven by an unquenchable hunger, he'll stop at nothing.

Book 3: Forsaken

Gwen's rescue from David Holmes is only a respite. Her older brother Sean was dragged into the entanglement with Holmes and was almost killed. Sean Jones places all the blame for his injury and the trauma his sister suffered at Keira's feet. To him, Keira's nothing more than a talented dilettante, with just enough power and knowledge to make things worse.

Having regrouped, David Holmes begins a campaign to terrorize all of those Keira loves. He has one demand—for her to join forces with him to obtain and exercise even greater power. Against the advice of those she loves, and against the critical, scornful disdain of Sean Jones, Keira forsakes her life to try to corral and defeat Holmes

At the last minute, her strategy is thwarted by a group of women who rescue Keira and give her safe harbor. She is introduced to an ancient organization, The Illuminata.

Their mission is to provide a haven for children born with extraordinary abilities. These children are known across the world as 'Indigos'. Sometimes they've been revered, other times they've been persecuted, but Indigo Children are a special lot.

Keira is astonished to learn that her childhood and youth of not really being able to 'fit in' is shared by many others. One young Indigo, Esther, is a miniature Keira. Just as headstrong, just as impulsive, they've got more in common than differences. Thankfully, they develop a close relationship before they kill each other.

But Holmes isn't going away. He manages to track Keira to her sanctuary at The Abbey. In a demonic rage he demonstrates his capacity for harrowing evil in an unspeakable act.

The Illuminata flee The Abbey and Keira's left to try to find them. The deeper she looks into their leader Cora's history, the more frightened she becomes. Is Cora Gaines truly a guardian of these children? Or is she an agent for others bent on controlling them? With Sean's reluctant assistance, she finds them. Only to be shut out again. What is Sean's connection to Cora Gaines anyway?

Ascendant

Keira now faces the greatest challenges of her life and struggles on all fronts. Family, friends, loved ones are all at grave risk in this final climatic episode.

All of her questions will be answered...but at a cost.

One

I WAS MISERABLE WAKING UP; but looking back, that was the best part of my day. Before I could barely get a coffee into me I confronted a horror so bad, it was like something you'd only read about. The hurt and confusion in my heart was completely eclipsed by the news that came through the door shortly afterward.

When my eyes slowly scraped open after only four hours of sleep, the events of last night came to me like a movie trailer.

After searching for Esther along the windswept Irish coast—that pain-in-the-neck, fourteen-year-old I wanted to take under my wing—we found her late at night. Gwen, Sean, Roy and I located her at some kind of sanctuary operated by the Illuminata. They were 'protecting' her and a gaggle of other kids behind a barrier of energy. An energy field, though unseen, made their hideout not only invisible to others, but somehow made regular people not even notice anything weird.

My stomach rolled as I stretched out to silence my phone's alarm. The violent nausea I'd experienced when I reached out with my own abilities and encountered that barrier was a troubling memory. It had driven me to my knees, puking my guts out like a high school kid on New Year's Eve.

But then Sean, with a single finger, disabled that...*thing* and waltzed through it like it didn't exist.

How the hell did he do that? popped into my head for the hundredth time since last night when I sat up in bed. I'd never seen him display any kind of ability like that before! And the son of a bitch wouldn't tell me!

He wasn't teasing me, either. He was being *secretive.*

Sure, we found the girls right after, and Esther was perfectly fine. And no... my efforts to foster her were once again thwarted by that bitch, Cora Gaines.

As severe as "The Church Lady," she was in charge of the bunker the kids were in. More than that, she had put the kibosh on my plans to become Esther's foster parent. Twice.

She was a big shot with the Illuminata, the person who had uncovered Blackwatch's plan to kidnap all the girls. Those kids had all kinds of special talents that would make Harry Potter green with envy. Well, maybe a dark blue, because that's what the girls are. There's a legend about them, if you dig deep enough: Indigo Children. Mostly female, they're known to possess otherworldly gifts. With some it's ESP, others have a skill at telekinesis, some are clairvoyant and on and on. They all share one common quality: they all emit a strong aura of deep blue—indigo.

Living with the Illuminata they were in an environment where they were accepted and nurtured in exploring their gifts. Blackwatch wanted to weaponize them.

Cora didn't believe that I had the maturity to look after Esther, and since she was a minor, a ward of the Illuminata, I was stonewalled. I had already tried and failed miserably to hire lawyers and investigators to get a court case for custody. No lawyer would take the case in Dublin, and the investigators came up empty in finding the Illuminata's offices.

My antipathy for Cora went into hyperdrive last night when Sean appeared. As soon as she laid eyes on him Cora transformed into a simpering schoolgirl. A simpering, frumpy schoolgirl who was almost my *mother's* age! I found out that those two had a history from years back when he lived in Toronto. What *kind* of history though? Guess what—yep, another Sean secret.

Coming out of the shower, I considered a bleak future without the girl and dismissed it out of hand. I wasn't giving up this easily.

I had managed to wheedle a final visit with Esther later this morning back at their sanctuary. The great and powerful Cora had decided that since we found them, their position was no longer secure, and they were going to relocate somewhere in Europe. The way she looked at it, if a rich kid like me, with the 'marginal talents I demonstrated' was able to not only locate their position, but get past their defenses, what could an organization of thugs like Blackwatch accomplish?

And Sean agreed with her!

Oooo! I toweled my hair with a vengeance. I really had thought there was something between Sean and I! But when Cora rendered her decision, there was no hesitation when he nodded his head agreeing! Not even a peep on my behalf!

I came out of the bathroom wrapped in one of those super luxurious terry robes the hotel provided. Hell, with what I was paying for the room it was the least they could do. I eyed my clothes sitting in a dreary pile on the floor when a soft knock came from the door.

"Yoo-hoo!" Gwen's voice came through. "You awake? I got coffee!"

I glanced at the clock--seven fifteen. Damn, I love that girl. Best friend, compadre in my work shepherding lost souls, and she's up early enough to get me coffee! I swung the door open. She stood there—farm girl, fresh as a daisy—a smug smile under her stunning gray eyes. She held up both hands. In one was a take-out tray with not one, but *four* Venti's with the familiar white and green logo. In her other hand she held a shopping bag.

"I got you fresh clothes," she said, walking into the room. "And one of these coffees is for Roy, and another is mine." She looked around the room; her eyebrows arched.

"Two for me will be fine!" I said. I took the tray from her and she pulled my new clothes out of the bag, draping them across the back of the love seat in the suite.

"I had to slip a fifty to the manager to open the boutique early," she said.

I glanced at the price tags. Holy shit—at those prices the place should be open twenty-four seven! I shrugged, though. Right now convenience counted for a lot, and I had felt really grimy when we checked in last night. And what the hell, with the inheritance left to me by Nana I could buy the hotel lock, stock, and barrel should the urge strike.

A full casual outfit, including underwear and socks, was laid out for me.

"I also added to my own wardrobe. You're going to have a whopping series of room charges," she added with a titter. Gwen knew how much I was worth; hell, she was with me when the lawyer told me. I waved my hand dismissively. "Oh, and Roy needed some things," she grinned.

I sighed and turned to her. "And your brother too, I suppose. Yeah, Sean, the guy I was all twitterpated over is her older brother. Go figure.

Gwen looked around the room, question marks on her eyebrows. "You mean he's not here?"

I shook my head. "No… and there would be *no way* he'd be in here after how he took Cora's side last night!" I had booked three rooms for the four of us when we checked in. I knew Roy and Gwen would sleep together; they'd been an item for a year now. But Sean and I had barely kissed up to this point, and what happened last night had put the brakes on anything more.

Well for now, anyway.

Honest.

Gwen's face had a puzzled look. "He's not in his room, and I didn't see him downstairs in the restaurant when I picked up the coffee."

I waved my hand. "Maybe he's down in their gym, or taking a swim in the pool… I don't know, and I don't care."

"That doesn't sound like him." She shrugged. "Well, you get got two coffees, then, I guess." She turned to the door. "You coming down for breakfast?"

"Yeah, I just want to call Shaniqua at the bunker. We're heading back up there as soon as we can."

"You want one last goodbye with Esther, huh?"

My lips set. "Not a goodbye... more of a 'see ya soon.' I'm not giving up, Gwen."

"I got you," she said, nodding. "We'll figure this out." And was gone.

I threw on my new clothes and stuffed the dirty ones into the shopping bag. I hadn't even bothered opening my suitcase. I grabbed my phone and hit speed dial.

Shaniqua was one of the three women I had first met from the Illuminata. They had operated a place known as The Abbey for the twelve girls. They defended me during my confrontation with David Holmes, a crazy old man who wanted to enlist me as his sidekick in some mad plan to destroy The Veil. And in so doing, the head of The Abbey, Zara, was killed which led to Cora showing up and taking over and moving the kids to that bunker on the coast.

Did I mention that the crazy old man, now on life support because of a stroke he suffered in the melee, is my grandfather? Yeah, I know... if it sounds crazy to you, imagine what my head's like.

Shaniqua answered on the fourth ring. "Keira? I was just about to call you." Her words came out in a breathless rush.

Oh no. My heart leapt into my throat. "Why? What's up?" Had Blackwatch, found them?

"It's Cora. She's missing. I don't need to tell you how dangerous this is. I feel like we're sitting ducks after last night. I still don't know how you guys got through the barrier, but you did, which means someone else could too." I could hear the fear in her voice. "Cora took the car two hours ago!"

"What the hell is she up to? Is she on their side?"

There was a pause. "I... I don't *think* so..."

"Don't move, we're on our way!" I disconnected and ran from the room.

I flew into the restaurant. Gwen and Roy were sitting near a window all snuggled up.

"That was fast!" Gwen's smile dropped when she noticed the expression on my face. "What's wrong up?"

Roy stood up, about to pull my chair out, but I ignored him. "It's Cora. I just spoke to Shaniqua. Cora's disappeared. I told her we'd be there as soon as we could. Let's go."

Roy cleared his throat, and his voice was low. "Sean's gone with the car."

"What!" My gut sank like a stone hearing my suspicions confirmed. They were together. "Great." It was bad enough that he'd snuck away to be with her, but the timing for the girls couldn't be worse. The Illuminata were trying to protect the children, and Sean and Cora were putting them in jeopardy. "We'd better get a taxi. It would be the fastest."

Gwen looked past me. "I don't think we'll need to."

Two

I TURNED AROUND and Sean stood there, his hands jammed into the pockets of his leather jacket. His eyes flitted from me, to Gwen and Roy, and back to me.

"Where are you guys off to?" he asked, his gaze fixed on me.

"As if you didn't know." I sighed. "We're heading back out to where the Indigos are. Their fearless leader, Cora, has disappeared, and I think she's up to something."

"She's not up to anything. In fact..." He glanced at his watch. "By now she's back with them and they've left for Europe."

"So you *were* with her." When he gave a slight shrug, I could have strangled him. "Couldn't let the morning go by without spending time with an old flame, huh?"

"Keira—"

Roy coughed. "I think I need to water my plants." He stood up and took Gwen's hand. "Don't you agree, babe?" In no time flat they made themselves scarce leaving Sean and I alone at the table.

I spun back to him. "So they're *gone*." He nodded. "What about Esther? You *knew* I wanted to see her again!"

He drew in a breath. "There wasn't time, Keira." He pointed at the table with his chin. "We need to talk."

My mouth dropped open at the tone of his voice. I'd used it a couple of times myself, and I heard it from guys once or twice in my life. It was the 'I'm dumping you' tone. Flat, but with a tinge of sadness. I couldn't believe it. Cora shows up, and he's throwing me under the bus!

Don't be an idiot, Keira! echoed in my head. Yeah, we're able to project thoughts to each other. Sometimes it comes in handy. I shot him a look. He shook his head, looking at me like I had just done something stupid, his finger pointing at the table. *Just sit down. This is way bigger than your love life, okay?*

"Damn right it is, mister. You helped that bitch rip Esther out of my life!"

He blew out another huff of air and took a seat. Keeping his eyes on the tabletop, he held up a finger. "First of all, there's absolutely nothing going on between Cora and me that's a threat to what you and I have."

"But you *do* have a history."

A small smile formed to soften his face. "I guess you could say so, but not how you think." With a sharp nod, he added, "I've known her for ages, though."

"Oh, *ages* huh? You're not even thirty!"

He lifted his head and held my gaze. "Take my word for

it—ages."

I was willing to give him some leeway over Cora… hell, I *wanted* to believe him, I know. I could shelve that for now. Still, I folded my arms, staring down at him.

He held up a second finger. "Furthermore, Esther… and the rest of the kids are gone for damn good reasons that I agree with." He gestured at the table. "*Now* will you sit down?"

"Damn good reasons, huh? Like what? Is Blackwatch hot on their tail?"

"No." He looked off to the side. "In fact, they've pretty much given up on the whole thing. When your grandfather was taken out of the picture, their money dried up."

"Now I'm confused. So right now there's nobody hunting the Indigos."

"That's right."

"But Cora, and the rest of the muckety-mucks in the Illuminata have to hide the kids in Europe anyway."

"Yeah."

"*Why*? This doesn't make sense!"

"Because they're still in danger… in fact, they're in more danger now than they were when they were being hunted."

"Who the hell is it this time?"

"It's not just the kids, Keira." He looked around the busy dining room. "The whole world's in danger. Right now."

I gaped around the restaurant half expecting to see some gang of terrorists burst in. "What the hell are you talking about?"

"Cora told me we're on the brink of Armageddon. And I believe her."

"Armageddon."

He took a deep breath, "Yeah... the Apocalypse is about to start."

"What the hell do you mean?"

He lifted his head and looked me straight in the eye. My mind was filled with *exactly* what he meant.

From above I was looking down on Manhattan shining in the autumn sun. In an instant it was blotted out by a white burst of light. From the center of this massive fireball, pulsing waves of energy flew out for miles, obliterating everything in its path. Majestic office towers, steel and stone bridges, apartment buildings and warehouses, every single thing for miles was blown apart like they were made of cardboard. People at the center of the blast were vaporized in the blink of an eye, but those miles away—miles and miles away—were burned alive as if they had stood in front of a flamethrower. With an unrelenting, unforgiving force, this nebula of horror stretched out across the city and surrounding metropolis faster than the speed of sound.

Miles away from the blast was the real horror; those who didn't die instantly suffered in agony before succumbing. I saw screaming, melting faces, burned flesh smoking as people rolled in agony. Cars, trees, telephone poles and small children, tiny *babies* were sent flying from the shockwave before the superheated inferno behind it overtook and consumed them alive as they shrieked in agony.

With a mercy, the vision went black.

My knees went out from under me, and I lurched to the table. Sean leapt up and helped me into my seat.

Armageddon.

Three

SOMETIMES YOU CAN JUST GET TOO DAMN CLOSE to something, and this vision Sean planted in my mind was a perfect example.

Let me explain something about these kinds of visions. It's not like watching a movie, okay? You're not watching, you're right in the middle of it. It's virtual reality on steroids. I could not just see and hear what was going on, I was experiencing the pain and fear. It wasn't watching a horror movie, it was *experiencing* it.

Weak and drained, I sat at the table gasping for breath while he rubbed my back, apologizing.

"I'm sorry, Keira. I thought you'd be able to handle it!"

My head hung forward, trying to catch my breath and swallow bitter bile that had surged up into my throat from the awful scene. Not just awful, though.

Truly horrifying.

I looked at him. "Is that a prophecy? Is that going to happen?" Barely managing a whisper, "Nuclear war?" All that crap my parents had told me about was ancient history, not something that could actually happen! They would go on and on at times telling me about how when they were younger everyone was so scared of it happening! "I thought we got rid of those nuclear weapons! Wasn't there an arms treaty or something?"

"No, there's plenty of them out there. They can't kill everyone ten times over now, just three times," he sighed.

"Oh. Well that's a comfort. Not!"

I sat up straighter when the server appeared with a look of concern on her face. "Are you all right, ma'am?" she asked.

"I just got some bad news, I'm afraid. I'd like a Bloody Mary please." Sean jerked next to me. "Make it two, if you don't mind."

Her mouth hung open for a moment. I don't blame her. It was a Tuesday morning, barely eight a.m., and here I was about to start drinking. But I have to tell you, I really, really needed a drink. And if Sean didn't want his, I'd down it, no problem.

When the server left, I turned back to Sean. "Well? Is this going to happen or not?"

"It's a real possibility, yeah."

"Oh shit, Sean! When?"

He shook his head. "I don't know. Pretty soon, though. This kind of foretelling by the Illuminata means it's on the horizon." He shrugged. "If it's true, that is."

I slapped my hand on the table. "Now you sound like you think it's all bullshit!"

He got a faraway look in his eyes. "I'm confused. I know that I really *don't* want to believe it, okay? But on the other hand, the Illuminata are pretty damn powerful when it comes to mystical things… and, well, Cora's really sure it's going to go down." He shook his head slowly. "I'm not one hundred percent on board, but I'm sure not going to blow it off."

The server brought our drinks, and I took a long pull. "Well, you pretty much nailed how I feel about all this," I shrugged. "Either way, there's nothing I can do about it, so I'm still going to find Esther." I watched his face. "With or without your help."

He scoffed. "What the hell is it with you and that kid anyway? You spent a month under the same roof at The Abbey, and now you're all stoked to be… to be what, exactly? Her fairy godmother or something?" He pushed his own full drink away. "I mean, why not one of the other girls? Why *any* of them for that matter? I don't get this."

I stared at him silently. I wasn't surprised he didn't get it; I didn't understand it fully myself. When Esther and I first met at The Abbey, the boarding school operated by the Illuminata, it was hate at first sight. We were like oil and water. She was a sullen twelve-year-old with a nasty streak who thought I was a spoiled, rich kid who got anything and everything handed to me on a silver platter.

But in the course of that month, each of our layers of defenses peeled away one at a time. And at the end of it all, I saw more of me in Esther than I ever had in anyone else. And she saw the kind of young woman she would like to become. I'm not all that good at explaining stuff like this, but I realized, right down to my core, that I needed her in my life as much as she needed me.

And I wasn't giving up on her.

Oh! Now that you put it that way, why didn't you just say so! I snapped a look at Sean seeing the smug look on his face. I didn't even feel him reading me! I cuffed his upper arm. "Cut that out!"

He ducked back. "Well, at least I kind of get it now," he chuckled.

Taking his hand in mine, I leaned closer, "So you'll tell me where Cora took her?"

He sighed. "Look, I promised her I wouldn't. How about you just trust me that she's as safe as she possibly can be?"

When I took his hand, I felt that familiar energy pass through both of us. From the first time we touched each other, it was there. It was a warm pulsing surge that came over me, and seeing the look in his eyes, he had the same sensation.

But he still wouldn't tell me, and his mind was as closed as Fort Knox!

"What hold does that woman have on you!" I tried to fling his hand away but he wasn't having any of that.

Giving my fingers a squeeze, he answered, "Nothing like what's between you and me, believe me."

"Then why are you taking her side in this!"

His shoulders dropped. "She doesn't trust you."

"What!"

"Hey! Think about it! When you came into contact with the Illuminata, what happened? Your grandfather was right on your heels, and Zara was killed, right? Well, Zara was a very dear and close friend to Cora."

"She blames *me*? You're kidding! Look Sean, it was the Illuminata that came to me! I had never heard of them before!" Which is true. I was on my way to meet with David Holmes in order to keep him from harming my family. The price was that I was to join him in some crazy goal of world domination or something. I had no intention of doing that; my plan was to neutralize him somehow, and ensure the safety of my loved ones. But my plans went up in smoke when the Illuminata entered the picture. They squirrelled me away from him for a while, letting me stay at one of their homes: The Abbey. That all blew up when Holmes tracked me down.

He killed their leader, Zara…who was, unbeknownst to him, a daughter he never knew about. And then he suffered a stroke; one of the kids did that to him right after Zara was murdered.

David Holmes now lay in a hospital bed, a drooling old man not aware of his surroundings. I also discovered that he had been under the influence of some demonic power up to the moment of his stroke. That demon was now gone, and Holmes is a husk.

Sean held his peace as we stared at each other. "Look," I said, "Zara's death weighs on me too, you know! Sure, Cora knew her longer, but she was my aunt! She's my mother's half-sister for Pete's sake. So Cora can get off her high horse, Sean. Blood's thicker than water, you know."

"I know, I know… but that's the way it is. Cora's erring on the side of caution, Keira. To her, we're in perilous times, and she sees you as increasing the risk." He held up his hand. "I tried my best to get her to see it differently, and maybe in time she will—like you and Esther came to see each other differently. But for now, she's the one legally obligated to look after all the Indigos, and that's what she's decided."

My eyes narrowed. "You're still taking her side over mine!"

"Damn it! I'm not! You're being stubborn!"

"Well, I'm staying on, here in Ireland, Sean. I'm going to try to see if I can hire people to find them."

"That hasn't worked out too well for you so far, Keira."

"No thanks to you."

"That's bullshit. Just remember, I was the one who got us past their barrier the other night, right?"

"I'm not giving up." I remembered something my parents told me just then. I had another card I could play. We stared at each other.

He took a deep breath. "You're very hard to like sometimes, you know that?"

"Look who's talking."

He pushed his seat away. "This isn't getting us anywhere." He stood up. "I'm heading back to Canada. You're not going to get anywhere trying to find Esther—the Illuminata are *that* good. But you're not in any danger anymore...and I have to see someone back home."

"Another old flame?"

He barked a laugh. "Nope. A biblical scholar."

"Whaaat?" He was talking in circles, going from the witch Cora to a biblical scholar.

"Yeah, when Cora told me about the prophecy, she mentioned some stuff from the Bible—the book of The Apocalypse. I happen to have a good buddy who's a known scholar on that specific topic back home. I'm going to go see him and see if there's anything more to what she said."

He bent over and kissed my cheek. "You and I are going through a hard time right now... but it will pass. I'll see you back in Kingston."

And with that he left.

Which was good, because I didn't want him to see me cry.

Four

I WIPED MY TEARS and took out my phone. Scrolling my contacts, I found Inspector Kreely in England. He was a tremendous help in rescuing Gwen when my grandfather kidnapped her.

I shuddered before I hit the dial button. My grandfather David Holmes had been a powerful manipulator of paranormal energies—as powerful as my Nana had been. Their common traits were what had brought them together, and my mom Susan was the result.

David and Nana never married. In fact, she left him as soon as she realized she was pregnant back in the nineteen sixties. Nana didn't know it at the time, but David had fallen under the ever increasing influence of a demon. A demon committed to seeing the destruction of The Veil, and the resulting universal chaos that would ensue.

How much of David's evil was due to this demon, and

how much was of his own intent is anyone's guess. After having kidnappings, attempted murders, and the outright murder of another daughter—my Aunt Zara—he suffered a massive stroke.

It was Inspector Kreely who helped smoke him out, so naturally it was Kreely I was contacting to help me locate Esther.

Considering how much I had complicated the man's life, I wouldn't blame him if he refused to answer. With fingers crossed, I placed the call.

"Keira Swanson! What trouble are you in now, dear!" His British accent, as mellifluous as Prince William's, came through the speaker. I immediately felt better.

"You know me too well, Inspector," I said.

"What is it this time? Hobgoblins? Poltergeists? Or something as run-of-the-mill as a kidnapping?"

I couldn't help but laugh. The man was a charmer. "Nothing so earth-shattering, Inspector. A simple case of finding a child."

"A child? A missing child? Dear me, that's serious, Keira."

"No, Inspector…she's quite safe. *Quite safe?* I'm speaking to this guy for ten seconds, and I'm already sounding like Mary Poppins! "She's a young girl I've taken a shine to, who is a ward of an organization that I'm trying to locate. They've moved her somewhere in Europe, and I was hoping you could help me out." I took a breath. "You actually met her, Inspector."

"Oh?"

"She was a student at that school where the headmistress was killed."

There was silence on the line. "I see. Bloody business

that…" He paused. "It's interesting, Keira; I remember the episode, of course… terrible event. But…"

"But what?"

"My memory's quite fuzzy on that event."

"What do you mean? David Holmes? The dead woman Zara? You're having a hard time recalling all of that?"

He chuckled over the phone. "I'm afraid my age is catching up with me…" He paused.

I waited in silence.

"Refresh my memory, would you? I'm sure there are case files here. I'll pull them up and reread them… or something, I suppose…"

His voice faded again. What the hell was happening now? Kreely had been with me through thick and thin, and now he was having trouble recalling this?

He cleared his throat. "Now, let's take this from the beginning, shall we, dear? A child is missing. Where was her last known location? Who was in charge of her care? Was it a Children's Aid Society or something?"

"Uhhh… no. Not exactly."

"What organization is this, then?"

I took a deep breath. "They're called the Illuminata."

"The Illuminati? As in the Knight's Templar? Or is it the Freemasons? That organization?"

"No! This is primarily a woman's organization. It's spelled similarly, but ending with an 'A' not an 'I.' I heard his keyboard clattering away. The man must already be in his office. I leaned over my phone. "You don't remember meeting them?"

I could tell he was somewhat flustered from the sound of his voice. "Vaguely… I suppose… Hmmm… I'm not getting any hits on such a group. You're sure that you gave me the correct name?"

"Absolutely. I know they exist. They own a mansion and grounds called The Abbey in Ireland! You were *there*, Inspector!"

"Somewhat out of my jurisdiction, now. I work for Scotland Yard in the U.K., Keira. What would I be doing in Ireland?"

This was bad. Real bad. Kreely and I had been involved in tracking down Holmes when Gwen had been kidnapped. Wait…

"Inspector… do you recall our adventure on the Isle of Man?"

"Of course! Like it was yesterday! Your friend Sean had been wounded. Your other friend… his sister Gwen if I recall, had been abducted!"

"But you don't remember The Abbey? And David Holmes?"

There was another pause. "That *is* odd, isn't it? I do, but only in the most vague sense."

Something had been done to him. The Illuminata somehow had shrouded his memory.

"Is there another abduction, Keira? Like with your friend Gwen?" His voice was full of concern.

"I'm not sure, Inspector. The girl… her name's Esther. She was at The Abbey when you met her and the rest of the children!"

"The Abbey. A boarding school…" I heard his keyboard clacking in the background. "Hmmm… I'm coming up with no such location, Keira."

"What?" I gave him the address again to confirm, and he did a search on Google Maps while I held.

"Curiouser and curiouser, Keira. The image I'm looking

at shows vacant farmland. Are you positive that's the correct address?"

"Yes! I spent more than a month living there! That's how I met Esther."

"Really? Hmmm… well, as usual, my dear, you've certainly piqued my curiosity once again!" His voice dropped low. "Is this going to turn into another escapade such as we had on the Isle of Man? That was quite surreal, wasn't it?"

"I don't think so, Inspector… but the way your computer's behaving… well, I thought it was going to be a simple case of finding a missing person."

"Well… how about this; give me all the information you can about this child, and I'll see what I can come up with. Where are you?"

"I'm in Dublin Ireland right now."

"Can you arrange to see me later today? My shift ends at four."

I stared at the phone in my hand. Kreely's office was in London, England. I sighed. Well, another plane to charter, no doubt. "You can't just phone me?" I asked.

Let me just say that jet-setting around the world isn't all it's cracked up to be, okay? Sure, I could afford it, no problem. But just to let you know, I don't have my own private jet; I have to go through the rigamarole of chartering them every time…and it's a real pain in the neck.

Okay… not nearly as bad as flying commercial, but give a girl some sympathy, all right?

"Hmmm…" Kreely paused on the phone. "No. I think in any event of dealing with you, Keira, it's best if its face-to-face." He barked out a laugh. "You have carfare?"

"*Yes Inspector,*" I said, dripping sarcasm. "I have carfare."

"Wonderful! See you at four! You can stand me a pint then!"

***

Okay, with all my whining, it really was a piece of cake getting a plane to take me to London. I was there in less than three hours.

I had some time to kill, so I did some mad shopping at Harrods and had them ship my purchases to my home in Kingston. I got the cutest outfits!

At four on the dot I was at Kreely's office. There was some kind of uniformed receptionist at the entranceway who looked me up and down quizzically. Kreely was older than my dad, and my showing up right at his quitting time made her curious. I didn't need to read her mind to know that—I only did to confirm my suspicion.

What's this American Hollywood type got to do with the Inspector? echoed in my head.

'Hollywood type?' She thought I looked like some famous actress? I could have kissed her!

She stepped through a banker's gate into a large bullpen and made her way to a glassed-in cubicle at the end and knocked before entering. In a moment, she stepped back out and gestured for me to come in.

"Thank you so much," I said as I passed by her. 'Hollywood type' was just what my ego needed.

My mood deflated the moment I entered the office.

Inspector Kreely looked at me with his face set in stone.

"Miss Swanson, I believe?" he said.

"Inspector? What's with—" I shut up when he lifted a finger to his lips, his eyes intense now. "Yes, Inspector, I'm Miss Swanson."

"Pleased to meet you. Take a seat, please."

I parked myself in one of the two chairs in front of his desk. As I smoothed out my skirt, I probed his mind as he leaned over the desk making a 'shushing' gesture. *For the love of God, girl, keep your mouth shut! Damn, I hope she's smart enough to pick up on my hand signals.*

No, he didn't have the slightest idea that I could read his thoughts. So I just sat and looked at him with questions in my eyes. I wasn't going to try to communicate telepathically with him; if I did so I was afraid the guy would totally freak out. He was scared enough as it was, judging from his thoughts.

"Well, Miss Swanson, your odd request about this… Illuminati organization was a total waste of my valuable time, you know."

When I opened my mouth to correct him, he slashed at the air, his eyes like lasers.

"Frankly, I need to ask—are you under the care of a psychiatrist?"

What the hell? "No!"

"Well, Ms. Swanson, I believe that you ought to consider consulting with one. Your request was outlandish, you see. The Illuminati is simply a men's organization of fellowship, you know. They certainly *do not* traffic in children!" He laughed weakly. "Dear me… that's like accusing your own country's Rotary Club of being involved with drug smuggling!" He let out a laugh.

"But—" Again his hand slashed the air and I shut up.

"I should have known when you made a reference to the phase of the moon during our conversation on the phone."

My mouth dropped open. I hadn't said anything about the moon. He slashed the air again, and when I probed his mind, I caught the thought that he was trying to have me sound like I was crazy... *for my safety*. My mouth slammed shut and I nodded slowly. "Well, when the moon's in phase, then the cats speak to me, you know."

He let out a sigh that *sounded* exasperated, but was really one of relief. It was at that moment I realized he was worried that his office was bugged. Oh man... He lifted his hands, palms up. "Sadly, you don't appear to be a threat to yourself nor to anyone else, so I can't take you into custody." He dropped his hands to the desktop. "You're simply a very addled, and quite delusional young woman."

My mouth dropped open when he stood and stepped to the door of his cubicle, opening it. "I believe you should avoid phoning the police the next time you have one of your episodes, Ms. Swanson. Good day." He held his hand out the door, gesturing me to leave.

My face flamed. This was outrageous. What the hell happened? I stood and brushed past him and left. I eyed the woman at reception, who kept her eyes on her desk as I went out the door.

Hollywood type echoed again in my head and I caught a small smirk on her lips. Bee-yotch!

When I left the building I walked down the street and turned the corner. I walked three more blocks and went in and out of several stores, each time looking behind me.

When I was satisfied that I wasn't being watched, I opened my hand to read the note Kreely snuck into it as I left his office.

RED LION GRILL AS SOON AS YOU CAN

was written on it.
What the hell?

Five

I T WASN'T HARD to get directions to the place from a passerby, and I was there a short time later.

It was a boisterous British pub. The bar was packed to the gills with people having a pint after a day at the office. I scanned the crowd and didn't see Kreely at all. I continued through the bar to a room behind it. At the very back I saw Kreely peeking around a doorway of another private room. As soon as he saw me, he made a sharp wave and retreated inside.

"What the hell was that all about, Inspector?" I was practically yelling as I shut the door behind me.

He was seated at a table for eight, with two empty pint glasses in front of him, and took a long pull on a third. "I have no idea, Keira." He bent to the side. "You're sure that door is closed?"

I slapped my hand against it. "Yes, it's closed!"

Silently, he gestured with his cell phone in one hand and held his other out. I didn't need to be Sherlock Holmes to figure out what he wanted. I took my phone and fiddled with it, removing the battery. If you've seen as many episodes of *Homeland* as I have, you'd have known right away what he was doing. Okay, I read his thoughts too—but just to confirm, okay?

"Very well... now I'm as confident as I can be that we're alone." He glanced around the room. "This is a private room, the pub's owned by my best chum from childhood, so I'm confident we're not being listened to here now that both our phones are inoperable." He dumped his own phone and its battery on the table beside mine.

"What the hell's going on?" I plopped into a chair across from him.

He leaned across the table. "Your friends the Illuminata are quite powerful, and quite adamant about remaining secret, Keira."

"You were calling them 'Illuminati' back in your office! What the hell was that all about!"

"I was covering my ass, dear." He let out a huff of air. "Listen to me, and listen closely. As soon as I got off the telephone to you, my computer stopped working. Completely. It shut itself off, and I was unable to turn it back on."

"That's weird."

"It gets stranger. No more than five minutes later, my phone rang. It was a summons from the office of the head of detectives! I was instructed, in no uncertain terms to report to his office immediately." He sighed. "Granted, it was only an elevator trip up to the thirtieth floor, but still… I've never, ever been summoned there before! I'm just a low-level inspector, Keira; there are many, many steps in the chain of command between my level and the head's office."

His voice was shaky as he said it.

"Go on…"

"When I arrived, I was ushered into an interview room. There were two men, in black suits, wearing sunglasses who asked me a few questions about why I was so interested in the Illuminata." He looked from side to side. "Dear Lord, I knew that there was something up, and that it could prove to be heinous to my career!"

"So what did you do?"

"I laughed, of course! I told them that I knew a strange young woman who asked me to investigate some insane idea having to do with the Illuminati! I said you were a mentally unstable American woman from a wealthy and powerful family from across the pond I had met when I took my holiday in New York City. I told them that you seemed odd to me back then, and I was surprised that you were in Dublin." He shrugged. "I added that I knew you to be half off your rocker, and that I was going to have a sit down with you when you came to my office… try to get you to seek professional help for your delusions."

"What!"

"Keira! Listen to me! The world has become a much darker and more dangerous place! For years and years now, people with black suits and sunglasses are crawling out of the gutters and working for governments in the shadows." He made a sad smile. "Of course, their job is *to protect us* they'd say… but they serve other masters; they don't have the traditional oversight a simple policeman like myself has to answer to." He stared at me intently. "They're powerful, well funded, and if they decide to, they can make someone disappear—like that!" He snapped his fingers.

"Inspector, what's really going on?"

He dropped his head, shaking it slowly. "Forces are at play in today's world that are unseen." He looked up at me. "For example, The Abbey...where that woman was killed, and where those girls were housed."

My heart clenched. "Her name was Zara, Inspector. And she was my aunt." Just like my mother, Zara's father was David Holmes. She was the result of a relationship he had with a woman in Indonesia after my Nana left him. And she was murdered by Holmes's agents with as much consideration as swatting a mosquito. "What about The Abbey?"

He closed his eyes. "It's no longer there. If you did a Google Maps search of the address, you'd find vacant farmland."

I nodded. And if you went out there to see for yourself, you'd probably see just that. The Illuminata had created a barrier around the bunker they evacuated the girls to after Zara's death that made the place unseen to everyone but Sean—so why couldn't they do the same with The Abbey? "I'm not surprised, Inspector. They're quite powerful."

"Yes, yes..." He opened his eyes and leaned across the table. "But I don't believe that those two men I met at headquarters were working on their behalf, Keira. They exuded a blank malevolence that even a mere..." He chuckled and continued, "mortal such as me could sense." He shook his head. "No... they were from some other organization that has a bone to pick with the Illuminata or something."

"Like Blackwatch?"

"No... there are other forces at play, I'm sure of it. There's an unseen conflict for control. Control of what, I don't know, but a conflict... a war... is going on right now."

The prickling of the hairs on the back of my neck told me he was onto something. Just what, I didn't know, but there was *something*. "But you managed to fool those two guys, right?"

He sighed. "For the present, I suppose." He looked at me sharply. "My doing a search on the Illuminata triggered something. Just what, I don't know. I *do* know, however, that I rattled a cage somewhere. I managed to get out of it by claiming that you're mentally unstable, and that I simply made a typo in my web search effort."

"Did they buy it?"

He made a short laugh. "My hobby is that I'm a member of a local theatre troupe. I've played many, many roles over the years. I called on all of my skills and experience in performing to convince those two men that it was a simple misunderstanding." He nodded to himself. "Yes, I think they believed me." He looked sharply at me. "But...you *must* desist of any further inquiries in England. And if I were you, I'd leave England for a while as soon as you can." He chuckled. "You have the *carfare*, don't you, my dear?"

I nodded. I was going to wear out my American Express card before long.

"Keira, I think we'll have to part ways. Whatever it is that you're up to is dangerous... at least in England, but I suspect anywhere in the world. Whatever you're trying to do, I suggest you give it up."

As IF. No freaking way. I shook my head. "I can't,

Inspector. That girl needs me... and I need her." I already had a plan B in place anyway. It would require a trip back to New York.

"Well, good luck to you, then." He stood and took my hand in both of his. I felt a deep, fatherly concern from the man, and it warmed my heart. "You'll leave the way you came in, dear. I'll be going out the back entrance and through some alleyways."

I leaned over the table and kissed his cheek. "Thank you, Inspector."

I was going to have to bring in the big guns. I had to talk to Dad.

Six

LET ME JUST SAY THAT IT WAS A FLURRY for the next two days up to when our driver pulled up in front of the United States Senate in Washington D.C. Yes, I went back to New York to see Mom and Dad, and the next day we were arriving at the office of Senator Robert Kinsley, the senior senator of New York State.

Uncle Bob had been a friend of Dad's since childhood. His bestie, actually. They were roommates in college, and each was the best man at the other's wedding. When Uncle Bob decided to enter politics at a later stage in life—he was in his early forties and pretty late for a guy to start such a career—Dad and Mom backed him to the hilt with a couple million dollars.

In the social circles they were in, there's an element of

keeping up with the Joneses. To make a long story short, their contribution started an avalanche of contributions, and Uncle Bob became 'The senator out of the blue.' It turns out he's really good at it and quickly moved up in the ranks, to the point that now he's the Chair of the Senate Intelligence Committee in only his second term.

Because of Uncle Bob's stature, our limo was able to pull right up to the front of the majestic building. I gazed up at the dome of the Capitol and then to my left and right at the marble edifice that loomed over us. This building was the seat of unimaginable power—the most powerful nation in the history of the world. Okay, my knees shook a little.

"Pookie's not doing too badly," Dad said as we got out of the car.

I rolled my eyes. "Don't call Uncle Bob that, Dad. You know he hates it."

Dad waved with his hand. "I know, I know, don't worry." He turned and pointed to the distance. "Did you know that he's looking to change his address?" he asked, his finger pointing in the direction of the White House.

"The election's not for another three years!" I tugged at Dad's arm. "Besides, politics bores me to death, okay?" Dad lowered his arm. "I just want to find Esther."

"Yeah, yeah…" Dad shook his head. "You could work on being a little more impressed at how I managed to pull this off, y'know."

I stood on my tiptoes and kissed him. "Thank you Daaaddy!" I said in the singsong voice that was guaranteed to wrap him around my finger. "Now, where do we go?"

"Mister Swanson? Miz Swanson?" A man approached us with a smile. "I'm Brandon, Special Liaison Assistant to the Senator. I'm to bring you to his office."

I stared at the man, and my blood went cold. He was tall, fit, and in his early thirties. What got to me was that he was wearing a black suit. And sunglasses.

Dad was oblivious. I didn't tell him or Mom any of the details about Inspector Kreely; all I said was that I drew a blank in Ireland and needed help finding Esther. Dad shook his hand and Brandon led the way up the stairs to the main building.

He was smiling with perfect teeth, chatting up a storm with Dad about hockey and how much the Senator enjoyed visiting them in New York at their restaurant. He asked me how I enjoyed living in Canada. I figured he didn't know anything about my meeting with Kreely in that pub and relaxed a little bit.

But when I tried to probe his mind there was *nothing*. Not like the wall that Sean was able to put up; this was different; usually when I probe someone's mind I get a lot of background noise and their predominant thoughts at the moment. In Sean's case I would get an impression of a brick wall. But when I probed Brandon's mind... it was like he wasn't even there! I wasn't able to pick up anything at all.

He must have felt my effort, because he stopped for a moment and his head dipped lower looking at me over his sunglasses. "So!" he said with a smile. "Is there anything you're curious about on your visit, Ms. Swanson? Anything?"

"Umm... no, not really," I said. Dad watched the exchange a little puzzled.

Brandon clucked his tongue in disappointment. "You're not that interested in our nation's history, I imagine."

I shrugged. "No, not really... never did well in school."

"Hmmm... I may have heard something about that."

"Oh yeah? From where?" I was getting this guy's message loud and clear—we got our eye on you—which got under my skin. Sure, I flunked out a few times from a couple of schools, but to have this... this glorified security guard know that much about me really got my dander up!

Brandon made a small shrug and smiled again. "Why from the Senator, I suppose. He's done nothing but go on and on about you and your family since your father called, of course." We were heading down a corridor by this time, and he turned and gestured. "Well, here we are."

There was a brass plaque by a large polished wooden door that read Senator Robert Kinsley, New York and we entered Uncle Bob's offices.

I stopped dead in my tracks. It was a huge area, with a row of six or seven large desks that went down all of one wall. At the back of the office was a polished door with Uncle Bob's name on it.

You would expect a Senator's office to be a flurry of activity, with phones ringing and staff bustling here and there. You'd expect to see a waiting area stuffed with lobbyists, or reporters or whoever else is in Washington D.C. waiting for their few moments with such an important man.

Nope.

Uncle Bob stood leaning against the doorway of his inner office, with a wide plastic smile on his face. His teeth were showing but his eyes were hooded. There wasn't another soul in the office.

Except for a second guy. In a black suit. Wearing sunglasses. He leaned against the desk closest to Uncle Bob's office. His arms were crossed across his chest as he watched us enter.

"Richard and Keira Swanson, as I live and breathe! It's great to see you guys!" Uncle Bob called out. "Get over here and say hello!"

Dad was oblivious to the emptiness of the office and charged right up to his old friend, pumping his hand. I almost stumbled crossing the bullpen behind him. Who were these guys? When I tried to probe the other guy's mind, I drew another blank. And got the same quick smile as I did from Brandon. Uh oh.

Uncle Bob gave me a quick hug, told me what a fine woman I was growing into—as if I was still sixteen and not twenty-four!—and ushered us into his office. But before he could close the door, the guy who was leaning against the desk stood and put a hand on the edge of it.

"I'll sit in on this one, Senator," he said.

"Who the hell are you?" I asked.

Uncle Bob's eyes flew open wide. "Now Keira, this gentleman assists me. He was a lot of help in our efforts to locate your little friend." He looked from me to the guy and back before extending his arm toward his desk. "Of course you can join us, Brandon."

"Brandon?"

The guy kept his gaze fixed on me through the exchange. "That's right," he said.

"You're named Brandon," I lifted my finger pointing at the now shut doorway. "And the guy out there is named Brandon. What the hell is going on here?"

Uncle Bob tittered. Yes, tittered. In a weak, high-pitched giggle, he said, "Yes! Isn't that unique they would both have same first name! What are the odds, huh?" He hustled across behind his desk and sat in the huge leather office chair. "Please, have a seat! I have a committee meeting scheduled and I'm already late. This won't take but a moment."

I grabbed Dad's arm before he could sit down. "I don't think we need to, Uncle Bob. You weren't able to find out anything, were you?" I shot a look over to the other man who nodded slowly, with that same small smile he gave me when I tried to probe his mind.

Uncle Bob watched me and that other Brandon carefully. "Well… no, not really, Keira." He shook his head sadly. "I contacted several of my colleagues in the intelligence community and none of them were able to discern anything about that organization your father told me about."

"The Illuminata," I said.

"Yes." Uncle Bob looked over at the Brandon guy who was standing by the doorway. "These gentlemen interrupted their own busy schedules to conduct research at the deepest levels and were gracious enough to take the time to report to me personally."

I turned and looked at the guy. "I'm sure they did."

I could see his eyebrows arch behind the sunglasses as he smiled again. He gave a small shrug. "Sorry, but they don't exist."

With my arms crossed in front, I leaned in. "Oh really? My, my, that sounds familiar for some reason."

The man stepped from the door toward me. "Oh? And why would that be? Have you made other inquiries?"

My breath caught in my throat. Before I could think of a reply, the guy continued. "When you were in England, wasn't it the Illuminati you were searching for?" He glanced up at Uncle Bob and back to me. "Now it's the 'Illuminata,' isn't it?" He made a sort of 'tsk tsk' noise. "You need to make up your mind, Ms. Swanson." He held his hands out in front of himself, palms up. "You've been quite a distraction on both sides of the Atlantic, you know." He pointed a finger at me. "So much so, that your friend, Inspector Kreely——"

"What did you do to him!" I snapped.

"Calm down, miss. He's fine. He simply decided that it was time for him to take his retirement from the police force." He cocked his head to the side. "So soon after seeing you, and——" He snapped his fingers and added, "like that, his career..." He turned his head toward Uncle Bob, finishing with, "ended abruptly."

We all stood in silence as I watched Other Brandon win a staring contest with Uncle Bob, who looked away and licked his lips nervously.

"Daddy?" I said, taking my father's arm. "I think we've done all we can here. I wanna go home."

Dad looked down at me, then at Other Brandon and over to Uncle Bob, who nodded silently. "Yeah, sweetie, I think you're right. Let's go."

Other Brandon's face bloomed into a smile as he reached behind him and swung open the office door.

We left silently and didn't say another word to one another until our plane lifted off heading back to New York.

Seven

W E DIDN'T TALK VERY MUCH on the flight back to New York either. Dad had a car waiting for us at the private plane terminal at LaGuardia Airport. When I got in the back of the limo, he signaled me to stay quiet, so I held my tongue on the trip home.

We went through the front door and I turned to him. "Can we talk about it *now*?"

He nodded. "Yeah. Let's get your mother first." He looked back out the side window of the entranceway and nodded again. "I didn't know that driver, Keira. Nor did I recognize any of the crew from our plane. God knows, your mother and I use those companies enough times that we are familiar with all the workers…"

"You think they were spies? Like the Brandon guys back

in Washington?"

"I don't know…" He straightened up and looked over at me. "And not knowing for sure is enough to make me be careful." He shook his head slowly. "What the hell's going on?" He turned to me. "This is a lot more than you trying to get custody of Esther, isn't it?"

"I don't know, Dad. Those two guys… I don't think they were with the Illuminata."

Mom's voice called from the parlor. "Keira! Richard! We have company!" I heard her giggle. "Or… well, Keira's got company!"

I went into the parlor and there was Sean, standing by the fireplace, holding a glass of water.

"He arrived just a minute before you two," Mom said, smiling like the Cheshire cat on the love seat.

"Hi Keira," Sean said. He looked like I felt. There were dark circles under his eyes, a stubble beard, disheveled hair, and his clothes looked like he had lived in them for the last week. I peered at him closely. Waitaminnit. Those *were* the same clothes he was wearing four days ago back in Ireland!

"What the hell happened to you?" I asked.

He dropped his head and gave himself a once-over. "Yeah…" he said, brushing his hands over himself, "I'm pretty road worn, huh?" He let out a weak laugh. "Unlike some people I know who can charter planes and limos, I've had to rely on normal transportation. Since Ireland I've been to Rome and then Toronto and now back here."

"Rome? Toronto? Doing what?"

He glanced at my parents, then back at me. "Is there a place I can talk to you alone?"

"We're outta here, guys," Dad said. He held his hand out to Mom. "Susan? Let's make sure the plants are watered in the kitchen, okay?" He and Mom made themselves scarce.

Sean flopped into the love seat and patted the cushion beside him.

"Okay, what?" I said when I sat down.

He took a deep breath, "I'm pretty sure that Cora's right."

"About what? That I'm not fit to look after Esther?"

He shook his head. "No. About the other thing—the reason they took the girls to Europe. I think they're right that there's a storm coming... Armageddon."

"As in end of the world?" A chill went through me. That's exactly what he meant.

"I went to Rome to look into something I had heard about. There was a saint who made a series of prophecies about the pope a long time ago, and I wanted to check out his writings at the Vatican."

"What saint?"

"His name was Malachy. He lived in the eleven hundreds in Northern Ireland. Apparently he had visions, and he even made predictions about the times we're living in."

"Like what?"

"According to Saint Malachy, there would be, all told, one hundred and twelve popes. He even was able to name them, or at least identify them from their coat of arms. He said that Pope Francis, the current pope, is going to be the last." Sean chewed his lips. "His writings are kept under lock and key in the Vatican and I wanted to see them for myself. It took a little doing, but I managed to read them."

I looked at him skeptically. "Oh, so you just managed to waltz into the Vatican, to their library of writings by saints, grab a chair and read to your heart's desire, huh?"

He pulled a face, drawing his lips back. "Well... kind of.

It was a little more involved than that, but basically yeah; I went in and read the stuff I needed to." He waved his hand. "How I did it isn't important. What's important is what I learned." He let out a huff of air. "From Rome I went to Toronto to see my buddy—"

"The Biblical scholar."

"Yeah; Father Bob Grippo."

"Sounds like the name of a Mafia hit man."

He shrugged. "That's his name, and he's a good guy. He's fluent in the ancient languages and has done a lot of work on the Apocrypha."

"Apocrypha? Now that sounds like the name of a skin rash."

He shook his head. "Nope; they're ancient writings that for whatever reason weren't included in the Bible as we know it today. Some of that stuff's really out there— prophecies and foretelling—and Bob has studied them. He thinks…"

He paused and looked at me. "He thinks that there's going to be nuclear war really, really soon. And it's going to start with North Korea."

"Oh get real, Sean. People have been saying crap like that for some time now."

"No… not *these* people, Keira. In its entire history of more than a thousand years, the Illuminata has *never* bought into end-times theory. My readings of Malachy's actual writings can't be disputed." He wiped his face with his hands. "And I've never seen Bob Grippo so… so scared."

I jumped out of my seat and put my hands over my ears. "Stop it! Stop it! I can't hear this shit!" My hands dropped and I stared at him. "This is some crap cooked up by you and that Cora bitch to keep me from getting Esther!"

"You self-centered twerp!" He jumped up and stuck his face in mine. "If you think for one minute that's true, you're crazy!" He took my hands. "Look, in case you haven't noticed, I'm crazy about you, okay? Sure, I've known Cora for ages and ages, and yeah, we're close; but that has nothing to do with how I feel about you, all right?"

From the second he touched me, and that rolling wave of energy joined us, I knew he was telling the truth about how he felt.

And about everything else too.

I looked into his eyes. They were usually a pale sky blue, but now they were darker, almost a bluey-green color, like the ocean during a storm.

"So that's it? We're a couple now, and the world's going to end?" I felt elated and terrified at the same time. It sucked.

"Maybe we can fix this," he said.

I let go of him and laughed. "Yeah, right! You and me… we're going to stop North Korea from starting a nuclear war!"

"Well, the way it was explained to me, is that North Korea's going to launch a nuke at the U.S. Who will respond with a shitload of nukes back at them—like a hundred missiles in retaliation for them launching one."

"So? It would serve them right!"

"Next, you're going to say 'they started it,' right?" He looked at me like I was a little child. "The North Korea missile would have gone off course and landed in the ocean." He held up a finger. "But then, out of the hundreds launched at North Korea, a few of those will lose their way and land on China instead." He tilted his head at me. "How do you think they'd respond?"

The air went out of my chest. "They'd hit back."

"Hard, Keira. They'd hit back very, very hard. And before you know it, Russia's launching, England's launching, France's launching... even Israel is going to launch. Missiles and cruise missiles are going to be flying all over the place, killing billions and billions of people, Keira. Pakistan will launch at India, who will respond... everyone in the world with a nuke will push their buttons the second they get scared enough."

"And you think that we can stop this from starting." When he nodded, I hissed at him, "While the great Illuminata is hiding, we're the ones who have to stop it!" He hung his head as he nodded. It hit me right then—"Is Esther going to be safe?" When he nodded, I said, "Where is she, Sean? Where is she that you're so sure that she's safe?"

"I can't tell you, Keira. I promised."

I reared back and slugged him. Right in the side of his face, I hit him as hard as I could and knocked him over.

"You bastard!" I shouted. I took a breath and continued, my voice low. "You want me to figure out some way to stop the damn world from ending, but it's more important that you keep a promise to old Cora!"

Mom and Dad rushed in from the kitchen. Mom stopped in her tracks, seeing Sean getting up to his feet, rubbing his jaw. "Keira, what did you just do?"

"What I should have done ages ago," I said. "He needs some sense knocked into him."

They all stared at me.

"Let's get some ice on that, Sean," Mom said. "Keira doesn't do it often, but she packs a heck of a punch." She gingerly touched the side of his cheek. It was welted but good. I already knew that because my own knuckles were skinned and my hand hurt like hell. Did you think Mom was worried about my hand? Nope.

Dad stepped over to me and lifted my hand, opening my fingers. "Move them," he said. I flexed them and he grunted. "Well, you didn't break any *this* time," he said with a small smile. "We heard the shot from the kitchen. I hope you didn't knock any teeth out."

"It'd serve him right." I flexed my hand again. It stung like anything.

All at once I felt drained, completely empty. I pulled my hand back. "I'm going upstairs, I'm taking a hot bath, and I'm going to bed, Dad."

When his eyes flew open and he glanced back to the kitchen, I waved at him. "You and Mom can figure out what to do about Sean. I'm going to bed."

Eight

I CLIMBED THE STAIRS TO THE SECOND FLOOR. I needed a bath, and a good night's sleep. But more than that, what I needed was some time alone.

To pray.

Well, not pray, exactly. Even as a kid, I thought it was unfair to ask God to bring me stuff or get me out of trouble when I did something wrong. God has a lot more important things to worry about than the trials and tribulations of Keira Swanson; I get that.

I needed my Nana.

I took a warm bath, put on my pj's and I climbed into my old bed. Up until about a year ago it had been *my* bed, but back then my parents kicked me out of the house. Well, they really didn't *kick me out* per se... Ever since I finished high school, I developed this habit of either getting fired from jobs or flunking out of college programs. Anyway, after I was kicked out of acting school, my parents informed me that I was to move out and relocate to Nana's home in Kingston, Canada.

Up until that time I didn't even know the woman existed! But off I went, as if I had a choice! It took some time for me to even call her Nana. I called her 'GM' instead. Hey, sue me—GM was short for 'Grand Mother' okay? Maybe even 'Grand Ma' But she was the boss too, and if GM also stood for 'General Manager' so be it. Good grief, she came into my life like a speeding truck, so maybe General Motors was a better fit! Ha!

I'm so damn clever sometimes, don't you think?

Anyway, in that time I spent with her—that too, too short a time, I learned that she had incredible, mysterious powers.

The woman talked to ghosts for heaven's sake! She had a mission of some kind to help stubborn spirits of those who died to move over to the other side. To do so, they passed through a Mystical Veil. That Veil is the border between this world and the next, and her job was to look after it. Because if that Veil ever stopped working, the world of those who have passed on and the world of the living would collide.

And that would be bad. Not bad like a war or a plague. Bad like... well, like existence as we know it would shatter in the collision of two opposite realities. The reality of the living and the reality of the dead.

In other words, such a collision would bring about the end of the universe itself. That might sound a little over the top, but it's true. I'm able to deal with this responsibility because I've had time to get my head around it, but it's a fearsome burden, believe me. Nana told me that there are others in the world who do the same work, but I've yet to meet them. I've met the Illuminata, yeah, but they're concerned with looking after kids who show paranormal abilities at a young age. That was *so* not me! When I was a kid, my abilities were limited to playing The Legend of Zelda.

There are also other beings in our world who want to tear down The Veil and bring around this cataclysmic destruction. They're demons—evil beings that transcend our world and rejoice in the idea of destruction and pain.

One of them had possessed my grandfather David Holmes. Yeah, right now he's a vegetable in the hospital, but during the brief time I had known him he racked up a series of crimes involving me and those I cared about ranging from assault, to kidnapping, to ultimately murder. I never knew David Holmes before all this, and if I never lay eyes on that man again that'd be fine by me.

Thoughts of David Holmes, demons and the Illuminata banged around my head, clanged with Sean's message of Armageddon on the horizon and my encounter with the Brandon boys. How in the world was I supposed to sort all this out? How in the world was I going to be able to provide the good home and guidance I knew I could for Esther? So yeah, I was pretty jangled, despite the warm soak in the bath. I needed to get a grip, calm down, and center myself.

Pulling the bedcovers up, I closed my eyes and took a few deep, measured breaths, the technique Nana had taught me to center myself. I whispered a prayer, "Nana, if you're near, I need your help. I promise I'll get back to protecting The Veil, continuing your work, but I can't do it right now. I'm worried. Worried for Esther and..." I swallowed the lump in my throat, "... Worried that this might be the end. I need you."

Whether it was the breathing exercise or finally admitting my worst fears out loud, a sense of peace flowed through me.

I gasped as the scent of roses filled the air around me. That was her perfume! I felt a touch as gossamer as a cobweb brush my forehead—the only indication that I wasn't dreaming. When I opened my eyes she was next to me, a pale, gauzy figure gazing down at me with love. I reached for her hand but my fingers swept through the form.

Her voice filled my mind. *The Illuminata aren't entirely wrong. I fear that if nothing changes, the forces in play will destroy everything. The impact will be felt across the universe, across many universes, and The Veil will no longer exist.*

"Nana!" I said. "What forces? Is it the Illuminata? Is it nuclear war? What's with those Brandon guys?"

Her form just gazed at me silently.

"Am I going to get Esther?" At least she smiled at me then. That was hopeful, right?

"And Sean? What about him and that Cora woman?" At that question, she looked away. "Nana! What am I supposed to *do*?"

Tears spilled from my eyes and my shoulders wracked. I was only one person, and there was so much going on! The stakes at play were overwhelming. I felt a weight descend like an elephant sitting on my chest. It was up to me, but how? I hadn't the faintest clue where to start.

Trust yourself. You are so much more than one small being. Your power is allied to the force of good. That force is the alpha and omega, all knowing and powerful. The enemy knows that. It will stop at nothing to complete its mission. You, my dear, are a serious impediment. Be careful and trust yourself and trust your instincts.

"My instincts? What the hell are you saying?"

Rest now. The way will become clearer. Unfortunately, that's all I can tell you. Know that I love you, always.

And then she was gone.

Nine

WHEN I WOKE UP THE NEXT MORNING, I didn't even realize I had been asleep. Normally when I wake up I'm groggy and with a rancid taste in my mouth. That morning, it was as if I had just closed my eyes for a second after Nana's spirit left me. There was a cotton comforter draped over me that I pulled off to the side as I sat up.

When I headed into the kitchen, Sean was already there. He must have gotten a decent night's sleep, because he was showered, shaved, and had fresh clothes on.

He plucked at his shirt, a light tan number that fit him like it was tailored. "Your dad felt bad about you sucker-punching me and had this stuff delivered last night. The package was at my bedroom door."

Now, as every single time after I do something stupid, I felt… stupid. I closed my eyes and tucked my lips to the side. Inside my head I told myself to suck it up. With my eyes still closed, I said, "I'm sorry. I shouldn't have hit you."

"It's okay. I understand. My bad too. I should have told you that Esther's in Norway."

I opened my eyes, then squinted one closed looking at him. "Norway? If the world goes to hell in a hand basket, what makes them think that Norway will be spared? Isn't it really close to Russia?"

He shrugged. "I think the Illuminata know what they're doing, even on short notice. They've got a sanctuary inside the mountain on Spitsbergen Island. It's about as close as you can get to the Arctic Circle and still be accessible by commercial flights."

So they just decided to construct a mountain sanctuary. I thought you said they had never bought into all this 'end of the world' stuff."

"That's right. They've been at it for just a little over a year. It was sort of simple for them, though. There was already one there. Some rich guy back in the nineties constructed it. He was convinced that the world was going to end in two thousand and spent a fortune building the place."

"So… what, he just gave it to them?"

Sean shook his head. "No, the guy died of old age and the Illuminata bought it from his estate. They enlarged it so that it's big enough for them to look after the Indigo kids, and they're bringing in their memberships from all around the world."

I had to laugh. "The world's biggest slumber party!" The image of dozens, if not hundreds, of girls cooped up inside some mountain fortress was funny.

"It's a pretty big complex. They have everything on hand to ride things out for years."

"You're sure about that? Esther will be okay?"

He stepped over to me. "Everyone's going to be okay, Keira. You and me—we're going to stop this from happening in the first place." I felt that surge of energy again when he took my hands in his. I winced at the shot of pain from my knuckles as he held the hand I clobbered him with last night.

I looked into his eyes, and now they were that light blue again. I tilted my head and let out a sigh.

"What's wrong now?" he asked.

"My hand hurts like hell, and there's not a mark on you," I said sheepishly. "I expected you to have a black eye or at least a bruise."

He made a small shrug. "I guess I heal quickly or something, I don't know."

I felt a pulse of mental energy from him just then. Not a strong one, but it was there. He was being evasive.

I was about to say something when he asked, "So, what are your plans?"

"My plans? What do you mean?"

He tugged me close. "Your Nana didn't just pay *you* a visit; she also came to me. She told me that you would know what to do, and that I was to support you."

I felt the twinge of jealousy that Nana also paid him a visit. Okay, just a twinge; she's MY Nana after all. I brushed it aside and asked, "Isn't that Gwen's job? To be my Guardian?"

"That's when you two guys are working on helping spirits transition through The Veil. This is different."

Maybe he had a point. I heard my parents coming down the stairs from their bedroom. I tilted my head in the direction of the hallway. "Well, for starters, we're going to tell them what's going on."

***

Well, it was an interesting morning, to say the least. The thing that surprised me the most was how well they took the news that the world was on the brink of nuclear war. They didn't hesitate for a second in believing Sean's evidence; I suspect the fact that Nana visited both of us had something to do with that, and I said so.

"You guys wouldn't believe us as readily if we didn't tell you about Nana's visitations, would you?" I asked.

Mom looked at Dad, who nodded. She turned to me and said, "She didn't just visit you two last night."

Oh.

I couldn't even feel bad about that—she's Mom's mother after all, right?

Before I could say anything, Dad interjected. "She told us that unless you take this crusade on, it will probably come to pass."

Oh.

Mom continued. "So, we're in this with you. What do we do now? Your Nana said that we should follow and support your decisions."

Oh.

"Waitaminnit!" I said. "Why does it have to be me? Why should I be the one responsible for stopping this? There's the President, for Pete's sake!" When Dad snorted, I raised my voice. "Look! He's the damn President!" Before we fell into a political argument, I held up my hand. "What about the U.N. then? Why can't they stop this from happening?"

Dad got up from his seat at the kitchen table and put his arms around me. "I don't know why it's got to be you, baby girl." He brushed a wisp of hair from my forehead. "But..." He looked over at Mom, then Sean, and back at me. "But all of us are fine with it being *you*."

"Daddy..." I made a fist and tapped it against his chest. "I failed at everything for most of my life!"

"Yeah... well... kinda." His eyes were so full of love and pride when he said, "You've come a long way in the last year or so, haven't you?" He hugged me.

When he released me, I said, "Okay then. Pack your bags. We're going to Kingston."

"Okay... how come?" he asked. Mom had already stood up, but paused.

"The house. It's on those Ley Line things that increase my abilities. That's why Nana bought the place, right?" When my parents nodded, I continued. "So I figure if I'm going to come up with some kind of plan and get ready to take this on, my home base on Lake Ontario is where I need to be."

Sean took out his phone. "I'll call Gwen. She and Roy are already back there."

Holding up my hand. "Hang on a second. Rockets and missiles—they use computers, don't they?"

"Yeah, I guess... I mean... I'm no rocket scientist, but sure they do."

"Okay. Tell Gwen to buy a bunch of laptops. I have an idea."

"No problem. There's a wicked cool computer store right in the heart of the downtown. They got everything." He pressed a couple of buttons on his phone and put it to his ear. "How many should she get?"

"Start with a dozen of their absolute best ones. Tell her to haul ass and get them, and have them all charged up by the time we get there."

"Got it." He put one finger in his ear. "Hey sis, it's me. We're coming home, and you have some stuff to do." He turned and headed out to the living room.

"Dad? Call the car company, and the charter company at the airport. Have them put a crew together."

"Right." Dad pulled out his phone.

"Oh, and make sure it's a larger Lear, okay?"

He grinned. "In a hurry, huh?"

"Yep." I wasn't going to tell him how airsick I get in smaller prop planes. From New York City to Kingston in a Lear would just be an hour or so. Up... down and done.

Ten

I STOOD AT THE FRONT DOOR, watching as the shining black Cadillac DTS eased in front of our townhouse. "The car's here, Dad!"

Sean eased in beside me. "Sure beats hailing a cab," he said.

With a small shrug, I looked up at him. "We take taxis every so often, yeah, but Dad prefers using this company."

"Sounds expensive," he said.

I scoffed. "You want to know expensive? They also have a Rolls Royce limo. Now that sucker costs a bundle." Dad hired it for my senior prom because I nagged the hell out of him. It's a sweet ride. When me and the gang I went to the prom with pulled up to the school gym, we were the only ones in a Rolls.

"Keira… to me, a taxi's an extravagance, you know…"

I shrugged again and let out a sigh.

"What's with the sigh?" I felt his hand go up my back and a shiver went through me. I like the feel of his hand on my body. I've known this guy for months and months now, and just being around him got my motor running. We haven't had the chance to do anything about it yet, but boy oh boy, when the stars finally align, it will be *epic*. "Hey," he repeated, "what's with the sigh?"

Damn. I turned around slowly. "I grew up with this, okay? My parents are affluent—"

"And you're a billionaire in your own right."

I blinked. "No I'm not!" I'm close, yeah; Nana left me over eight hundred million dollars, believe it or not. In cash. Not in stocks, real estate or jewelry. I have a bunch of accounts, and when you add up the balances, it came out to eight hundred and twenty-five million bucks.

But not a *billion*.

Sean laughed lightly. "Where do you live now?"

I looked around my parents' house. No, I didn't live there. "In Kingston."

"Your applying for permanent residency, right?"

I made a wave with my hand. "The lawyer is handling that." Mr. Thompson looked after my money, taxes and all that stuff. I just couldn't be bothered. He also was the contact guy who provided Gwen and me with our assignments with looking after The Veil. "But yeah, he said that I needed to get that paperwork in order."

Sean crossed his arms. "Well, just so you know, in Canadian dollars, you're worth well over a billion." He reached out and nudged me. "Currency exchange and all that."

"Look, are you going to play 'working class hero' now or something? This is how I grew up, and I absolutely am *not* going to be feeling apologetic or guilty for it!" I jabbed a finger at him. "Sure I was born lucky, okay? But that's not my fault." I held up my hand. "Wait." I turned and looked at him. "Are you implying that I'm supposed to feel bad or something because I'm loaded?"

He licked his lips. "Uhhh… no."

"So what's your point, then?"

Now it was his turn to let out a sigh. "I don't know…" He pursed his lips. "I just think… that there are so damn many people in the world with… well… nothing, really… and this kind of wealth…" His voice faded.

As if growing up in New York, I've never had this kind of encounter. "Look, some people are born with advantages that others don't have; I get that."

"Yeah, well…"

Before he could go on, I added, "You have good eyesight and all your mobility, right?" When he nodded, I said, "Do you ever feel guilty if you see someone who's blind? Or in a wheelchair?"

"No…"

"Well, then why should I feel guilty? I don't, Sean." I put my hands on my hips.

"Well… then how do you feel?"

"I feel… *grateful* to tell you the truth. I see poor people, yeah. And in this city most of all, the wealthiest city on the planet… there're homeless people, people in poverty; that bothers the hell out of me. I pay my taxes, and I support politicians who think we can do better, but I don't feel guilty about what I was born into."

"So you're saying it was the luck of the draw."

"You know what I think? I think you're feeling threatened by the fact that I'm so loaded, and you can't impress me with stuff."

"Stuff?"

I nodded. "Yeah. Like a flashy car, or a nice apartment, or whatever. That kind of stuff." I shrugged. "It wouldn't impress me, and you know it."

He looked away. "I don't know what would impress you."

I scoffed. "You don't, huh?"

"No." He looked back at me. "Let's drop it, okay? We got bigger things to worry about than your money."

"You brought it up!"

"And now I wish I didn't."

"Whatever." I looked out the window. Eric, the guy we usually use to drive, got out and waved at me. He looked quite spiffy in his black chauffeur's uniform and cap. I hauled the door open and called out to him. "We'll be a few minutes, Eric!"

"Need help with luggage or anything?"

"We'll take care of it," Dad said, coming up behind Sean and I. "I don't want him inside the house or touching our things until I find out what happened yesterday with the company. Who were those other people and cars that we dealt with when we visited Uncle Bob in D.C.?"

I leaned back out the door. "We're good!" I called to Eric. "We'll be out soon."

He nodded, tipped his hat and stood by the driver's door.

I turned back to Dad. "You're still rattled over Brandon and Brandon, huh?"

Dad pointed toward where Eric and the car were. "And

the car service. And the flight company. Yesterday, everyone was new, right? And now it's back to normal. There's something going on there, Keira." He looked to Sean. "You know people in the Illuminata. Do they do stuff like that? Take over and put their own people in place?"

Sean shook his head slowly. "I don't think so… I doubt it was them. They're more focused on looking after Indigo kids, Mr. Swanson; not cloak and dagger stuff."

Dad nodded. "That's what I thought too. I had only met Illuminata members once or twice, and that was years ago." He gestured outside. "So until we find out more about what happened yesterday, we're not going to discuss anything about North Korea, or any of that stuff in the car or in the plane, okay?"

"Well," I said, "I can do something about that right now." I stepped beside the front door so I could look out the sidelight window beside it. I peeked out and focused on Eric, scanning his thoughts.

After about a minute, I turned back to Sean and Dad. "Nothing to worry about from Eric. He's thinking about how great it was to get a week's pay for *not* coming to work yesterday. He's not all that curious about it, other than he hopes it happens again."

"Okay, so he's clean, but the car might be bugged," Dad said.

Sean came up behind me and stared out at the car. "See if you can feel anything in that car that's recently installed, Keira."

"What, like a sweep? Do I look like the CIA?"

He shook his head slightly. "I don't think it was the CIA yesterday… just give it a try, okay?"

I unfocused my eyes and looked at the car. I tried to

sense if there was anything malevolent coming from it, but got nothing. "No, I don't think there's anything to worry about."

"You sure?" Dad asked.

"No, I'm not sure! I've never done anything like this before you know!"

Sean held up his hand. "Maybe, but your instincts are all we have right now to go on."

"In that case, *my instinct* is that the car's clean."

"That's good enough for me," Dad said. "Still, let's not be too blabby, okay?"

***

Eric did have to come into the house after all; Mom had packed four suitcases *and* a trunk! And that was just stuff for her and Dad.

"We don't know how long we'll be in Canada, Keira," she said. "I packed most of the things that are important to me. I asked myself 'if the house was on fire, what would I save?'." She patted the trunk. "All our photos and memories from when your father courted me, and your childhood are in here." She looked around the house, and tears sprang into her eyes. "God, I hope I'm just being stupid…"

"We'll get this fixed, Mom."

She started to cry. "Last night, after you went to bed, your father and I watched a TV movie from back in the nineteen eighties! It was called *The Day After*! It was about nuclear war! I saw it when I was still in high school and it terrified me!"

Shit, she was really, really scared!

She kept talking. "People were just going about their lives, and… and things got bad between Russia and the U.S.A… and the next thing you knew…" She put her hands to her face. "Everything was blowing up!" She dropped her hands and looked at me. Her eye makeup was running already. "Keira... we... I mean..." She waved her hands. "My generation *should have fixed this already!* But it's worse now than ever!" She started to sob again.

I glanced into her mind and felt such a cold stark terror in her that I started to cry. I reached out for her, and we both clung to each other. This was crazy. My mother's crying because we're heading to a nuclear war, and the only people we know who are trying to prevent it is us?

Is me?

This was beyond insane.

Eleven

IT'S A FUNNY THING. You get a plan in your head, and even when it looks like it's absolutely nuts, it's a damn sight better than sitting around the kitchen table bitching about what should be done.

We were in the Lear cruising toward Kingston, and everyone was sitting quietly. We were all in these super-comfy easy chairs with seat belts on them around a conference table, each of us staring off into space.

"Okay," I said. "We'll be in Kingston soon enough. Anybody have any ideas?"

"You have to get Gwen and Roy up to speed," Dad said.

Mom and Dad had been really quiet since her crying jag back at the house. They were sitting holding hands, their fingers knotted together like a lifeline. They both nodded their heads, and Dad spoke again. He pointed to Sean. "We have to tell your father too."

Sean nodded slowly. "Maybe I can talk Cora into taking him to Norway." He shot a look at my parents. "I mean, along with you guys of course."

Mom startled in her seat. "I'm *not* going to some hideout in a mountain while my *daughter* tries to break up—" She stopped when Dad shushed her. She threw his hand away. "I'm NOT!"

"For what it's worth, Mrs. Swanson, I'm pretty sure my dad is going to say the same thing." He snorted. "He wouldn't leave without his dog Buster, anyway." He turned to look at me, "First thing, we have to see just how well you can zorch computers from a distance."

I nodded. That was practical. "I should have tried in New York," I was a little embarrassed that I didn't think of it.

"Nah...I think learning how to do this in your house in Kingston, with the Ley Lines and all is the best place to begin. That way if you're able to, you're starting with a success. If you tried it in New York and it didn't work, then you'd be in...." He glanced over at Mom, whose eyes were red-rimmed and her face pale. "In an even rockier state than we are right now."

I could buy that. I nodded at him.

Mom's voice was low and plaintive when she spoke. "But then, even if it worked, honey, how would you find..." She glanced around the plane and said, "Those things?"

"I was thinking about that. I figure that I could Astral Travel and see if I can locate them that way."

Mom and Dad looked at each other. "You know how to do that, Keira?" Dad asked.

"Yeah. I did it in Ireland." My head fell to the side watching them. "You guys know about that kind of stuff?"

Mom nodded. "Your Nana talked to me about it. She did it a few times, but of course, I was never able to pull it off."

"Me neither," said Dad.

Sean's voice was low and hard. "No freaking way," We all turned to him. "That's shit's dangerous as hell, and *no freaking way* are you going to do it!"

My back stiffened. "Now you just wait a second!"

He slammed his hand down on the table. "No! You wait a damn second! I tried to warn you before, and we almost lost Gwen when you two did it the last time!"

He was right. Back in Ireland, Gwen and I Astral Travelled together, but got separated when we were in the spiritual dimension. She had been pretty much in a coma for a few hours before waking up. I shut my mouth.

"Look, Keira—you had a really close call."

"I was fine! It was Gwen who got in a fix!"

He shook his head. "Doesn't matter. When you do it... you're in the realm of spirits. You're not in your world; you're looking at this world, but through a window." He leaned across the table, his eyes hard as flint. "You're in the realm where demons are at their most powerful!"

"I didn't see any!"

"Doesn't mean they weren't there!" He sat back in his seat. "In fact, I think that your grandfather..." He turned to Mom. "Your father, Mrs. Swanson. I think that he became as terrible as he was because of Astral Travel. I can't see how the guy I met could have in *any* way been so attractive to your mother that she would have his child."

I waved my hand. "That was years and years ago, Sean. People change. Hell, look at how much I've grown in just the last year, right?" I looked at Dad. "Think about it! A year ago I was getting kicked out of school—"

"Again," Dad quipped.

"And now I'm on my way to save the world!"

Sean shook his head. "Nope. That's not the same."

"Why not?"

"You *grew* Keira. That potential was in you. David Holmes... I think he *changed*. He was possessed; we know that, right?" We all nodded. "I don't think he was that kind of a cruel, vicious man to start with." He pointed at me. "And if it happened to him, it could happen to you."

Dad waved his hands at us. "Settle down, you two. We're putting the cart in front of the horse right now. Let's get to Kingston, and first let's see if Keira could pull off this thing in screwing up computers. Then if that works, we'll figure out how to find..." He paused and looked around the cabin just as Mom did. "...Those things."

I burst out laughing.

"What's so funny?" Sean asked.

Holding my hand like a pistol, I pointed at myself, then him and then my parents. "Yeah. A college dropout, an office clerk, and some restaurant owners are going to save the world." I shook my head ruefully.

Dad snorted. "You left out Gwen and Roy! We've also got a letter carrier and unemployed pilot!"

Sean made a high-and-mighty face. "Well, in that case, we're good to go." We all burst out laughing.

The four of us were seated at a small conference table. Dad leaned forward and resting his chin on his hand, looked at each of us. "Never doubt that a small group of thoughtful, committed people can change the world. Indeed, it is the only thing that ever has," he said.

"Did you just come up with that?" I asked. It really sounded good.

He shook his head. "No, I saw it on a TV show years ago. Turns out it was said by a woman years and years earlier." He looked at me with an expression of pride and love. "And now there's a woman leading exactly such a group."

"Thank you, Daddy," my voice suddenly small. I glanced away for a moment, blinking to clear the film of tears that spread over my eyes.

I turned back to the table, and we sat there in silence for a moment, each of us carefully tending the small flame of hope that was lit.

I took a deep breath and let it out. "Look—I'm not planning on doing any Astral Travelling, okay?" I turned to look at Sean. "And if I do, I'll check with you first. Fair enough?"

Sean's gaze showed concern, but nodded. "Okay... fair enough." He dropped his hand below the table and grasped mine. Once again that feeling of warmth flowed over me. Damn! If my parents weren't here... I can't remember the last time I was so attracted to a guy.

If ever.

And it's been way, way, wayyy too long since I had me some hubba hubba time, okay?

What? A girl's got needs too, y'know!

I sighed. With my parents in the house... even if it's *my* house... I had a hell of a tough time seeing us getting enough privacy, no matter how solid the walls were.

Saving the world can be a real bitch, you know that?

Twelve

AS THE LEAR TAXIED up the apron in front of the Kingston Airport building, I saw Roy and Gwen standing behind the glass. I shook my head. It took us longer to get from my parents' home in Manhattan to LaGuardia Airport in Queens than it did for us to fly to Canada.

As the flight crew collected and stacked our pile of luggage—thanks Mom—the rest of us deplaned. It took a few minutes longer for Mom to get through Customs because of all the family mementos she had stuffed in the trunk. The poor bureaucrats didn't know what to make of it all: photos, preschool artwork, old dance class shoes didn't fit into any category of items they could check off.

Sean stepped in. "They're gifts from her—" He pointed

at Mom "To her."

The customs agent, a man older than Dad, lifted up my creation from Pre-K—macaroni pasted to construction paper with my name scrawled at the top with a pink crayon. "No commercial value, I assume?" he said with a smile.

"Just priceless, that's all," Mom quipped back.

The agent shook his head, closed the trunk and stamped the form. "Welcome to Canada," he said, waving us away.

In no time flat I was hugging Gwen and Roy. Gwen, Mom and I walked arm in arm across the airport lounge to the front door while the men got the luggage squared away. That was one good thing about a small airport. You could be in and out of there in record time, with a great parking spot.

At the car, Gwen held my shoulders, peering at me with clear gray eyes. "I haven't heard a word from you about Esther since I left you in Ireland. What's going on with Esther?" Her forehead lined with worry.

"Nothing, really. I hit a few brick walls and came up empty" I kept 'Brandon and Brandon' to myself for now. We had bigger things to deal with. "I *do* know..." I gestured at Sean, struggling with my dad to load Mom's trunk. "Thanks to Asshat Sean; Esther's safe for now in Norway."

Gwen's eyebrows flew up. "Norway? What the hell is she doing there?" She looked from me to my mother, then to my dad and back at me. "Keira? What's really going on?

"Bigger things than my desire to foster Esther."

"What?"

"Don't worry, I'll tell you all about it. At least regarding Esther..." I shrugged. "I know she's safe and well looked after."

"It's probably better that she's where she is for the time

being, Keira," Mom interjected, stepping up to us. I nodded.

Gwen opened the door to the huge SUV for me. As I climbed in, she asked, "What's with wanting all the laptops? I bought a dozen for you. They're back at your house."

Everyone else boarded and buckled up. Roy got in the driver's seat and smiled over at Gwen before starting the vehicle."Well, should we tell—"

"No, not now," she murmured, as she pulled the seat belt on. She then turned and her gaze flitted between Sean and me. "I'm dying to hear why we need all these laptops."

Sean shot me a weary look before beginning, "I'm afraid I've got some bad news. Well, actually Keira and I both do."

Gwen looked over my shoulder at Mom. "Is that why you came, Mrs. Swanson?"

"Yes."

Gwen looked at me. "Should I be scared?"

I nodded. For the next twenty minutes, the scenery of the lake skimmed by and the city was a blur as Sean and I explained everything that had happened. I watched Gwen's face turn pale, while Roy's eyes were wide glancing every so often in the rear-view mirror.

"Holy shit!" Roy was the first to speak after Sean finished. "I knew things were tense but this is crazy! Do you think we can actually stop this?"

Gwen's mouth had fallen open wider and wider as Sean had explained everything. Finally it snapped shut and her chin rose higher. "So the Indigos are in Norway? Nice of the Illuminata to stick around and help with this." She shook her head and blasted out a sharp huff of air.

"I know. That's kind of how I feel." Trust Gwen and I to be on the same page.

Gwen shot a pointed look at Sean. "What about this

Cora? If she was able to put up some kind of supernatural shield keeping their location safe, why isn't she here to help? We could use someone with her abilities."

Sean even managed to look sheepish, glancing at me before he answered, "I'm going to ask her. She was pretty adamant about staying with the girls the last time I talked to her. But this is too important, not just to them but everyone. If those nukes go off, we can all kiss our asses goodbye."

I snorted, "Well, she's *not* here, so we'll do what we can without her." Sure, help from *anyone* with paranormal abilities would be welcome. But I didn't *trust* Cora. Yes, she was with the Illuminata, but she also had worked for that private spy outfit Blackwatch. She said it was to get information on their efforts to locate the Illuminata, trying to use the Indigo children for their own ends... but how could anyone be sure?

Not that her old relationship with Sean had anything to do with my antipathy toward her. No! Maybe a little... "Cora's in Norway, in some kind of bomb shelter. We're here, and have a job to do."

Gwen looked at her brother. "What about Dad? Could you get Cora to take him in? Should we try to talk him into going there?"

From behind Sean and I, Mom quipped, "As if he'd go!"

Roy weighed in, "Your dad won't go, Gwen. If Keira's parents feel that way, then for sure, he won't want to leave. No. I think we're all in this together." He shook his head and was about to say something else, but looked at Gwen; his eyebrows a pair of question marks. When she gave a slight shake of her head, he stopped, never finishing his sentence. I turned to see if Sean had caught it, but he was staring out the window. Something was up with Roy and

Gwen.

I didn't want to, but my curiosity got the better of me, and I reached out mentally to her to see what was going on. Gwen and I had a huge fight a while back over me doing this, peeking into her thoughts, and I had really been good about giving her privacy, but sometimes... well...

But all I could sense was a cloudy miasma; not a single train of thought presented itself. Hmph! She was getting really good at keeping herself to herself. I backed off; the last thing I wanted was her sensing I was poking my nose where it didn't belong. Oh well, maybe later, she'd tell me. We were best friends, after all.

We pulled into the driveway of my house—more like a mansion—beside the St. Lawrence River and an eddy of sadness drifted through me. This was my Nana's home. I'd hated coming here when my parents threw me out, banishing me to spend time with her.

But everything had changed after meeting her. I looked to the side garden as we pulled into the driveway and smiled seeing the red roses blooming. That was where her ashes were. There was one rose bush in that garden that always had flowers, no matter the season. It was part of the strange mystery of the house.

Gwen turned before getting out of the car, "Do you want to start this thing with the computers right away, or are you tired from your trip?"

I laughed lightly. "We've only been traveling less than three hours, Gwen! I'm good to go." I shrugged. "Besides, we have to."

She clapped her hands. "I can't *wait* to see if you can pull this off!"

Sean leaned forward, placing his hand on the back of her

seat. "This is not a game, Gwen."

I hid the smile, seeing him assume the older-brother role. Gwen showed that she took it in stride. It showed the history of their close relationship. Older brother and kid sister. It only made me more aware of Esther and how I wanted her here with me. She was the closest I'd ever get to having a little sister. What was she thinking right now? That I'd forgotten her? I shook that train of thought off. There was work to do.

I looked up at the two-and-a-half-story stone house, the wide granite steps leading up to the front door. It was good to be home. From just over a year ago, hating every square inch of this place to this moment, feeling a sense of *home* looking at this stately manor, I was struck at how much I had grown. This was now *my home*.

Sean stepped over to me and took my hand in his. "Did you ever think when you first came here, you'd end up trying to stop a nuclear war?"

"You kidding? When I first came here and Nana introduced me to her resident ghosts, I thought I lost my mind!" I shook my head. "I thought ghosts were pretty scary when I first encountered them here."

"Yeah, and then you spent the last year herding them through The Veil." He shook his head slowly, a smile playing on his mouth.

"That was easy compared to this, thing, you know." He reached out and took my hand. I felt the heat of his hand and the surge of energy flowing between us. Like a shot of adrenaline, his touch increased my optimism that we could actually do this.

"C'mon you two." Gwen motioned from the top stair, holding the door wide. "Mrs. Turney was here today, and the fridge is fully stocked."

Mom came up behind us. "Good. Your father and I will look after supper then."

Gwen's eyebrows arched. "Really? She left a roast for tonight. Yorkshire pudding maybe?"

Mom patted her shoulder as she went past. "With roasted potatoes—no problem."

"Yum!"

Dad and Roy got the luggage out and were bringing them up to our respective rooms while Sean, Gwen and I headed in. I walked into the living room. Laptops were lined up along the buffet, plugged in and their screens glowing.

Roy called over as he and Dad carried Mom's trunk of treasures up. "I took all their floor models, because they were already up and running, is that okay?"

"Yeah, good idea." That way we didn't have to waste time getting the computers up and running. It would just be a case of charge and destroy—if I could pull this off.

Sean picked up a white Mac and then turned to me. "I never was an Apple fan. I think this one is going to be our first victim. What do you say?"

Gwen turned to him. "Maybe we should take it outside. You never know what will happen, right?" She headed down the hallway to the sunroom and then the back door, Sean and I following.

"You're ready to get to work, right Keira?" he said.

"Yeah. Let's give it a go." As we followed Gwen out the back, I looked around at the house. There was such a sense of my grandmother in the very walls around me. I glanced at the library where she'd spent her last days, too crippled to make the stairs anymore. I closed my eyes for a moment. "Nana, if you're watching, I could use a hand here."

With that I walked down the hall and through the sunroom. I didn't linger there. There were too many memories of the lessons and chats with Nana. Too long in there, and I would probably start bawling. Now was not the time for that.

The laptop was open on the patio table outside and Sean stood before it, booting it up. Gwen turned to me and smiled. "What now, boss?" She reached out for my hand. "Are we going to hold hands and try?"

In past escapades, when Gwen and I held hands, whatever psychic, occult, paranormal—whatever the heck it was that I had—those abilities became much stronger. I had assumed that I would need her with me when I tried this. I reached for her hand, then stopped.

It came to me out of the blue. I needed to try this alone.

"I'm going to try it first. If it doesn't work then you take my hand. And then if that still doesn't work, we'll ask Sean to join us. I need to assess this." When Sean stepped away, I stared at the computer, all the while breathing slowly, centering myself.

I'll be honest; I didn't have a clue how to begin. I mean, I didn't know any incantations, or spells or whatever. Not knowing what to do when you know you have to do something really sucks.

So I just stared at the damn thing, frozen in place and frustrated.

It started as a sizzle in my chest, expanding outward until my fingertips quivered, the power building. The laptop was about ten feet away from me. Closing my eyes, I focused all my thoughts on it. I imagined its inner workings becoming warmer and warmer—the motherboard, the hard drive and cooling fan. Hotter and hotter till smoke would drift from the keyboard. A flash of the nightmare of Armageddon flared in my head and then was gone, leaving a cold determination.

I opened my eyes and stared at the computer with a furious wrath.

There was a tap as the laptop vibrated on the glass surface. My fingers curled into fists and I lowered my chin, blotting out everything but the machine on the table. A pulse of power rose high in my body. I could feel it racing up my throat, through my mouth and then into my eyes. The laptop was jerking and banging on the table, and a tendril of smoke rose from the screen. A red flash of fire flared before the screen went completely black.

My jaw dropped.

Holy shit.

Thirteen

YOU DID IT! ALL ON YOUR OWN!" Gwen came over and gripped my shoulder. "Wow! I knew you could do it!"

"Nothing to it," I lied, buffing my nails on my chest. The edges of my vision had turned gray, and my knees felt a little wobbly. I stood there trying hard to appear nonchalant. The grayness ebbed back to normal and I sniffed, tasting a faint tang of blood in my sinuses. Oh boy.

"You sure you're okay?" Gwen asked.

"Yeah!" I nodded. "I'm just smoked that I actually did it!"

Sean passed us and went to the table. He went to pick up the laptop but yanked his hand back as soon as he touched it. "Ow!" He turned to us. "It's hot as anything." He made a grin, shaking his head, "I've heard of fried computers...but man!" He looked back to me. "Remind me to never get you hot under the collar at me, Keira."

I laughed lightly. "Just don't be an Asshat and you'll be safe."

"So what's next?" Gwen asked.

Sean held up his hand. "I think maybe see how well you can do over a distance? It's not like you're going to be able to sidle up next to one of those missiles, right?" He turned to Gwen, "Would you bring out a few more?"

As Gwen headed inside, I looked down the glen leading to the lake. "It's about one hundred feet from here to the dock. Why not try that?" After that touch of wooziness passed, I felt right as rain.

Gwen and Roy both showed up, carrying a few more laptops, which they deposited on the table. Roy stared at my first victim, thin tendrils of smoke wafting up. "Whoaaa..." He grinned, "that's one baked Apple, huh?" He looked over at me, his eyes wide with dawning wonder. "You did that? Seriously?"

"You bet." I tried to suppress the big grin that itched. "Can you bring the next one out to the dock? This time it's going to be a challenge."

Roy picked up a laptop and walked backward toward the waterfront for a few steps, "Just don't do anything yet. You make me nervous, Keira." But he smiled to show me he was joking.

"Let us know when you've got it fired up and then stand back." Gwen gazed at him with a shadow of worry in her gray eyes. She cupped her hands beside her mouth and called to him when he got to the end. "Maybe come back up here and stand by us?"

Roy waved her away. "I'll just keep clear!" He pointed at me. "Make sure your aim's good, okay?" He took two exaggerated giant steps back from the laptop.

Gwen's mouth twitched. "You're not gonna hurt him, right?"

"No. I focus on the computer, Gwen."

She sighed. "Okay... I just don't want anything to happen to him."

I rested my hand on her shoulder. "It'll be fine." I glanced over at Sean and saw him smile watching our exchange. Gwen had dated but she'd never had a serious boyfriend until Roy. But to give her credit, back when she was in her early twenties she'd been focused on getting her doctorate in physics. If not for her father's illness, she might have continued in that field. But he became sick, and she dropped out of grad school at Queen's University to become a letter carrier.

Sean was glad that she'd finally met the right guy. And if not for me, that never would have happened, so there! He was a charter pilot for the air company we used in New York City; no way he would have met her when she was living in Kingston and his base of operation was New York City. Who would have ever guessed when Roy flew me from New York to Kingston the first time that he'd end up working for me and in the process, meeting the girl of his dreams? It was sweet even if they were a quirky-looking couple—Gwen tall, athletic and gorgeous while Roy was stocky with a ready laugh on his round face.

I suppressed a laugh for probably the millionth time since they hooked up. Seeing them together made me think of Charlie Brown and Jessica Rabbit.

"Hey," said Sean. "You gonna do this or what?"

I fluttered my hand at him. "Okay, okay!" I closed my eyes, doing my breathing exercises. I emptied my mind of everything, centering my energy.

"Be careful of Roy, okay?" Gwen's voice was tremulous, standing close, but purposely not touching me.

A few more deep, slow breaths and my eyes opened. At this distance the computer was just a dark blip on the gray, weathered planks. Again, I saw in my mind's eye the components inside the machine, pictured them heating up as if sitting on a flame instead of the dock. I focused, blocking out any peripheral vision; Roy, the blue of the water, the green reeds at the shoreline. There was only the laptop.

My body tightened as I willed a searing white energy to the object. The same tingling rose through my chest and up into my head, pinpointing the energy into my eyes. But nothing was happening.

I took another deep breath and held it, pushing out the energy with all my might. Seconds passed. Then minutes.

"Let me help." Gwen's fingers curled around mine, but I yanked my hand away.

"No! I have to do this!" But why was this not working? True there was a greater distance but my energy still couldn't reach that laptop!

I shifted my focus slightly, the way I would do when reading a person's aura. The black laptop was now encased in an energy field of light. My own beam of energy appeared as a reddish beam that grew fainter as it neared the laptop.

It came to me like a jolt of lightening. The laptop's energy aura! That was what I had to destroy!

My body quivered, and for a minute I felt faint and dizzy. I closed my eyes and took a few breaths, all the while keeping the image of the energy field surrounding the laptop as sharp as I could. A pulse of electricity zapped behind my eyes, invading and becoming one with the laptop's. A buzzing sound filled my ears as the power in my head became stronger and stronger. It was sizzling hot, surging through my head, making my scalp tingle.

"Holy shit." Sean's voice barely registered.

I was magnetized, the power growing even hotter, a laser.

"Enough Keira! You can stop!" Sean's urgent voice broke through this time. I let my breath out slowly and then gasped. My heart was pounding and my palms were sweaty. When I opened my eyes, a trail of black smoke mingled in the breeze off the water.

Roy let out a whoop of excitement and then he waved his hands high in the air. He bent over the device.

"Don't touch it, Roy!" Gwen was a gazelle racing across the lawn.

Roy jerked back and called out with a wide grin. "Are you kidding? There's a freaking scorch mark on the wood next to it! No way am I going near that thing."

When Sean stepped over to me, I fell into his arms. This time, I wasn't near as perky or smug about my feat. I was drained. I let myself come down slowly, opening myself up to his strength. I was a sponge sucking every drop of his spirit into mine. He held me close, rubbing my back and shoulders. He didn't say anything, just let his own energy flow into me.

It was pretty cool, actually. I relaxed in his arms and closed my eyes.

In the darkness behind my eyes I could hear his heart thrumming in his chest with a steady lub-dub beat. I inhaled deeply, and over the top of his heartbeat I could hear *everything*. I heard the tiny skitters of the ants at our feet as they scuttled around doing their ant jobs, and at the same time could hear the whine of an airliner five miles above us as it passed overhead. I heard the pocket change jingle in

Roy's slacks as he droned onto Gwen about what sort of energy I unleashed. I could hear Gwen's teeth biting the sides of her cheeks as she tried to keep from laughing at him. I could hear the world around me in more beautiful detail than I ever could before.

And all these sounds came together in a melody of life.

The lightheadedness I experienced the first time was stronger this time. I wasn't worried about being unsteady on my feet though; Sean's arms around me kept me rooted upright. I sniffed again, and my eyes sprang open against his chest.

I glided my hand up his chest and flicked my finger under my nose, feeling the wetness. I looked down to see the sheen of blood from my nose on my fingertip. I quickly wiped my nose with my fingers, then the back of my hand.

"You okay?" he murmured.

"Yeah," I whispered. "My nose is itchy, that's all," I lied.

He grunted. "Means you're either going to have a fight or kiss a fool. My mom used to say that."

I checked my nose with my other hand and saw it was clean. I stepped away, stood on my toes and kissed his cheek. "Well, I guess I just took care of that, Asshat." I wiped my fingers on the back of my jeans.

Aaand, as if on cue, Mom came out the back door, breaking up the moment. "Keira? Is she all right, Sean?" She came up to us and her hand stroked my hair while her eyes were wide with concern.

"I'm fine, Mom. It worked. I think we can do this." And for the first time, I felt more hope.

It wasn't much of a nosebleed.

Fourteen

LOOK AT THIS!"

I turned at Roy's voice and saw him coming up from the dock, holding the dripping wet laptop, the plastic case wavy and warped in his hands.

"We had to splash water on it. It was in flames, man. 'Fraid you may have to replace a few boards on the dock, Keira. But holy Hannah!" He turned to Gwen, "She'd be great on a camping trip. No need to bring matches with this girl around!"

"Oh my God. YOU did this?" Mom nudged me and pulled me into her arms. "Oh Keira! If I ever doubted the wisdom of sending you to live with my mother, I don't have any doubts now." When she pulled back holding me at arm's length, there were tears in her eyes. "I'm so proud of you."

Dad had come out the back door of the kitchen where he and Mom had been putting supper together for later. He wore a cook's apron, and the sight of him reminded me of a younger version of Lawrence, my Nana's butler...and Guardian when she was doing work with spirits. He looked from Roy holding the melted computer and back to me, his eyes wide. My eyes met his, and I nodded.

"Hey Richard." Gwen stepped over to my father. "She fried that computer at a hundred feet. What do you think of that?"

I turned to look at Dad. His mouth had fallen open, gaping at me, his daughter. "Dad?"

His eyebrows bobbed to the sky and the 'O' of his mouth curled into a wide grin. "I'm blown away!" He shook his head slowly. "I've never seen you do any of this stuff, you know..."

I shrugged in a weak attempt to appear cool, but felt my face grow hot. I'd never seen my parents so thunderstruck. Sure, they loved me to death but... oh my God; they were in awe. Of me! My eyes filmed. It had been a long, long road, but my parents were finally, for the first time, *proud* of me.

Dad nudged my shoulder. "Hey... What's wrong?"

I shook my head. "Nothing... not a thing." I smiled and gave my head a shake. "Long way from getting kicked out of acting school, huh?"

His face went still, and he nodded slowly. "Yeah... yeah it sure is, ain't it?" He held out his arms and hugged me. "Atta girl, kiddo."

"Oh Daddy." I stepped over and snuggled into him, hiding my face. Tears were threatening to spill, and I didn't want them to see that.

Sean cleared his throat, "I think that's enough for today. Keira did incredibly well, but I think…" He eyed me. "Maybe a break is a good idea?"

"Yes!" I said. "Time for key lime pie!" I pulled back from Dad and grinned at Sean.

"Key lime pie! Of course! I'll go defrost one." Gwen turned to Roy. "Key lime pie is always the pick-me-up after Keira does one of her…" She paused. "Well, 'things' at any rate." She looked over at Mom. "Her Nana—your mother—started the tradition and whenever Keira and I do…"

"One of these things?" Mom added with a nod.

"Yeah." Gwen headed to the kitchen. "We always keep some on hand."

"Us Muggles can have some too, right?" Roy laughed and then put his arm over Gwen's shoulder. "I'll give you a hand."

I glanced at my parents and then Sean. "Hey, Sean; let's check out the dock and see how bad I scorched it, okay?" Mom and Dad got the hint and made themselves scarce while we wandered down toward the water.

I looked over at Sean. "Something's up with Gwen and Roy. Are you getting any kind of reading on that? Roy started to say something in the car and she cut him off."

His head tilted to the side, and he looked over his shoulder toward the house and then to me. "That's weird. Normally I can read her like a book, but nine times out of ten she blurts out whatever's on her mind before I *have* to. Did you teach her how to guard her thoughts?"

I shrugged. "Yeah, and I guess she's gotten better at it or something." I followed his gaze, wondering what was going on.

"Well, when they're ready to tell us, they will. For what it's worth, I'm not getting any bad vibes from either her or Roy."

I nodded. He was right. I turned back to Sean. "This…" I groped for a term. "Computer frying? I had a different experience from the last one."

He turned back to me. "What do you mean?"

"Just now, something happened with me. It was always when I'd get dizzy, that I'd grow. When I wrecked the laptop just now, I felt that. But what's weirder still, was the way I was afterward; I could sense everything. I knew Mom and Dad were coming out before they showed up. Mom came out. It was kind of… kind of an awareness of everything." I kept my nosebleed to myself. If it got worse, or if I got worried about it, I'd mention it then.

Sean eyes squinted, watching me closely. "An awareness?"

I nodded. "Well, more than 'aware'… I felt one with everything."

"What do you mean?"

I sighed. "I wasn't watching the ants at my feet, I…" my hands groped in the air as I tried to not just communicate the experience to him, but to understand it myself. "I… was kind of *being* the ants. I knew what the world looked like to them." I looked up at the sky. "There was an airliner flying overhead, and I knew what the world looked like for every person on that plane, all at once!"

He grew quiet. "I see."

I felt a little embarrassed. This sounded so stupid, hearing myself saying it out loud. I watched him watching me.

"Did it frighten you?" he asked.

"No! Not in the slightest! It felt…" Tears sprang to my eyes, and my voice became quiet. "It felt *wonderful*."

He nodded. "Yeah. It sounds that way." He took my hand. "Over in India they call it 'Cosmic Consciousness'."

"What, you mean like gurus and stuff like that?"

"I'm just saying that your mind expanding like that has been talked about."

"So you don't think I'm nuts?"

His voice was a quiet, soothing salve. "Oh Keira, noooo. You're not crazy… you've been *blessed*!" He took my hands. "Not too surprising that something like this would happen to you, you know. It sort of runs in your family, right? Your grandmother was pretty dialed into things beyond this world, and despite his failings, your grandfather too." He looked away for a moment. "And that's just for starters, I think."

We stood there holding hands at the end of the dock. I looked down at the scorched boards and tried to have that experience again, but nothing happened. Even so, I felt the silence between us comforting. He gets me, even when I don't get me.

After a while, we headed back to the house, holding hands. I've held my fair share of hands with guys… but Sean's hand in mine felt like no other guy's hand before. The connection between us—when he wasn't being Asshattery, that is—was something you could feel.

"I called my dad; he's coming over for dinner this evening. We'll need to fill him in on what's going on," Sean said in a thoughtful voice.

"Yeah." Devon is Sean and Gwen's father. Their mother died years ago, but her spirit lingers in their home. I've seen her just about every time I visited Devon, but for some reason, neither Sean nor Gwen are able to sense her presence, let alone see her. "I wonder how he's going to take this news."

"What? That the world might come to an end and you're going to stop it?"

"Well... yeah..."

Sean let out a snort. "I don't think he'll be surprised at all, to tell you the truth."

Fifteen

WHEN I SETTLED ONTO THE OVERSTUFFED COUCH in the living room the effort of the day hit me, and any energy I had drained from me. I laid my head against the back of the couch, exhausted. It came out of nowhere, and I closed my eyes just for a second.

"Keira." I blinked and jerked my head up.

"Oww!" What a crick in my neck! Gwen was standing in front of me, holding a dessert plate.

"You dozed off, and we decided to leave you alone," she said.

I rubbed the back of my neck, working the kink out of it.

"How long was I asleep?"

"About a half hour." She held the plate out to me.

I took the plate and fork and dug in. "Mmmm..." I said, taking the first forkful of key lime pie. It was now practically a tradition. Since Nana first began to teach me about things unseen: ghosts, The Veil, and its place in the universe, mind reading, telekinesis... all of her lessons with me ended with us sharing key lime pie. I looked over the comfortable living room and out toward the dining room, feeling Nana in every inch of the place.

"Thanks, Gwen," I said. After Nana passed, Gwen and I continued that tradition in our work together over the last year. I polished it off in no time flat and a belch slipped out.

She stood before me with her hands behind her back and an almost smirk on her lips. "Full? Or do you have more room?"

I tilted my head up at her. "You didn't!"

"Sure did!" She brought her hand around, and in it was my favorite, favorite comfort food. Thick chunks of melon, with extra large marshmallows over the top. I had just finished a slice of rich, tart pie, and my mouth started watering all over again as I reached out and took the dish.

"I died, didn't I?" I said as I dug in with the soup spoon. "Because..." I took a mouthful, and said, "I'm in heaven now!"

"Well, I guess blowing up high tech stuff gives you an appetite, huh?" she said. "I only gave you small portions because your parents are doing up a Sunday night style roast beef dinner."

"Don't worry," I said, talking with a full mouth. "I'll eat that too!" I was *ravenous*. I polished off the treat and put the bowl down on the coffee table before me, enjoying the sugar rush. I tilted my head at Gwen and patted the cushion beside me. "Take a load off; let's catch up," I said.

She sat down beside me. "Yeah, it's been ages since we talked!" she said with a laugh.

"Well, yeah! Four whole days after all!" Hard to believe that it was less than a week ago that we were all traipsing through Ireland searching for Esther and the Indigos. It felt like an eternity to me. I pointed at her with my chin. "But seriously... what's up with you and Roy? You guys have been kind of coy since we got back."

"Oh? You're curious? Why didn't you just read my mind?" she asked with a glint in her eyes.

"No. Freaking. Way." I said. When we had just began doing our work together shepherding hesitant spirits through The Veil, I had gotten on my high horse and poked around in Gwen's mind whenever I wanted. It didn't take too long for her to become infuriated with my disregard for her privacy, and we had a wicked fight over it. No way was I going to risk having that happen again. I shook my head. "Nope. I learned my lesson, Gwen."

She shrugged. "Try anyway. See if you can still do it."

She gave me a strange look—a challenging, smug look. I didn't have to read her thoughts to get the message that she was double dog daring me to try. "You sure?" When she nodded, wide-eyed, I said, "Okay."

I unfocused my vision and turned my head just a little so I could see her out of the corner of my eye. I reached out with my mind and sent a tendril of reception to hers.

Pixies and palaces, fairies and unicorns, laughter and tears...

I was taken aback, and blinked at her. She smiled at me.

It was a little strange; a chill went through me. I focused fully on her, and still...

The crescent, then the whole of the moon...

The images in my mind that I picked up were beautiful and innocent... and yet disjointed somehow. Like a picture puzzle where the pieces, although they fit, just didn't belong together. I peered at her, and she was smiling sweetly.

"How are you doing that?" I asked, stopping my effort and leaning back.

She blinked a few times, still smiling. "I came across a technique somewhere, and practiced it.

"Well, it sure works." I said.

She gave a quick nod of her head. "Good. Then there's no chance of us having an argument over your being too nosy then. I'm glad."

"Me too." But I also felt a sense of loss or something. Things were different between us now. Exactly what, I wasn't sure, but it was something.

Sixteen

GWEN'S DAD, DEVON, ARRIVED and Mom drafted us to set the table for supper. The smell of the cooking meal got my stomach growling again, despite having just had a huge snack.

As I took the plates from the china cabinet and passed them to Gwen, I said, "So... What's the big secret with Roy?"

She kept her eyes on the table, but there was a coy smile twitching. "What makes you think we have a secret?"

"You're kidding, right? You cut him off during the ride home, and both of you have been acting... well, *weird*."

She shot me a look. "Weird? What do you mean by weird?" I couldn't help but see a flash of annoyance in her eyes. "We're *not* weird!"

"Whoa…" I held up my hand. "Maybe weird's not the term. But you gotta admit, there's definitely something going on between you two."

Gwen's gaze slid to the passage door to the kitchen, where the sounds of everyone else chatting away filtered through. Her lips were a firm line when she looked back to me. "I'll tell you, but only on the condition that you keep quiet about it, okay?"

My hand flew to my mouth. "Oh shit. Are you *pregnant?*"

Her eyes widened in surprise. "No! What gave you that idea?"

"Well, what is it then, dammit!" I was really losing my patience with this cat and mouse.

She stepped over to me and took the rest of the plates from my hand and laid them on the table. "It's funny you mentioned pregnant, but I'm not. I *want* to get pregnant though."

"Whaaat?"

"I mean, I'm twenty-eight and all… I'm not getting any younger, and I need to have a kid."

"WHAT?" I couldn't help raising my voice. She shot me a look and shushed me. "Need to?" I never heard anyone put it like that—want to, sure—but need to?

Sean came through the kitchen door. "Everything okay out here?"

"Yeah," Gwen said. "Can you give us privacy?" When Sean looked at her quizzically, she added, "Girly stuff." And he backed right out of the room. She turned to me. "Whenever I say 'girly stuff' he thinks it's 'women's health issues' and gets grossed out," she said with a smirk.

"Gwen." I crossed my arms. "What's going on?"

Her voice dropped to a whisper. "Roy and I got

married!"

"WHAT!" Now I was yelling.

"Be quiet, Keira!" she snapped.

"But how... why? When? Where?"

"Well... we went to a justice of the peace as soon as we got back home from Ireland. It took a little bit of doing, but... well..." She patted her tummy. "I'll need my baby to be conceived under a sacred bond."

"That's the nuttiest thing I ever heard! I didn't know you were religious."

She got a faraway look in her eyes. "I didn't think I was either." She patted her tummy again. "But this is how it's got to be."

Mom came through the door. "What the hell is going on out here with you two?" she asked. "You scared Sean away, and now you're yelling, Keira. What is it?"

"Sorry, Mom." I eyed Gwen. "Gwen just told me that she's going to be backing off from helping me." Total lie, yeah, but I had to cover with something for Gwen.

"I didn't say that!"

"You said that you and Roy are getting really serious, right?" I shrugged. "I thought that's what you were leading up to." I dropped my eyes to her tummy. "All things considered," I muttered.

"Well, supper's ready, and we're tired of being banished to the kitchen," Mom said.

This was going to be one strange dinner. On top of filling Devon in on what we were doing and why, Gwen's whole secret marriage thing had me going from pillar to post.

Roy held the door open for Devon to shuffle in with his walker. The poor man has been battling MS for the last seven years. It was the reason Gwen left grad school to care for him. The life of an academic was a nomadic existence; even with a PhD, she would have to work up her resume until she could land a full-time, tenured position. That wouldn't work with her dad's health in such decline.

"There's something going on, Keira," he said as he took his seat. "Everyone has told me that the news has to come from you." He sat back in his chair, his eyes flitting over the rest of us. "I don't think you're going to be talking about baseball are you?" Since we met, the rivalry between the New York Yankees and Toronto Blue Jays had always been a topic between us.

I smiled weakly. "Well... I think the Yankees are still in the rebuilding phase...?"

As Dad carved the roast, Devon leaned forward. "Spit it out, kiddo, I'm not getting any younger. It's North Korea, isn't it?"

Everyone at the table froze and stared at him.

He let out a chuckle and looked from Gwen to Sean. "Your mother's spirit came to me last night. She told me that there is grave danger from North Korea and atomic bombs." He pointed to me. "And this whippersnapper is going to fix it..." He let out a sigh. "Well, *try* to fix it, she said, actually."

I leaned over. "Mary *communicated* with you?" I had seen her spirit at Gwen's home since I first visited. But I had never been able to communicate with her. I also didn't want to. Despite my mission of helping spirits transition through The Veil, I knew that neither she nor Devon were ready for that. He sensed her presence in their home, and I didn't have the heart to even try.

He nodded. "Yeah... it felt like it was a dream, but she

was pretty specific."

Sean huffed a sigh. "Why are *you* able to contact her but not me?"

"Or me," added Gwen. She shot a look at me. "You're able to see her, but we're her kids!"

"Can it, you two," Devon said sharply. "That's the way it is, for whatever reason." He looked back to me. I hadn't seen him in a few weeks, and he had lost weight, and his hair had turned from ash gray more toward white. Even though the disease was taking its toll, his eyes were still sharp. "So what's the tale, nightingale?"

We told him the whole story. How the Illuminata had concluded that there was going to be a nuclear exchange between the U.S. and North Korea in the near future, my new ability to fry computer components, and the hazy outline of our plan—disable North Korea's missiles.

"Why not just take out their leader?" he asked. "I mean... the guy's squirrelly as hell, isn't he? He had his brother murdered, right?"

"Not to mention what he did to his uncle," Roy added. "They say online that he had the guy killed with a handheld rocket or something. The guy's definitely nuts."

"No!" I said. "I'm not going to be some sort of assassin."

"It would save a lot of trouble, Keira," Devon said, watching me carefully.

"Really? For whom? I'd have to live with myself for the rest of my life, and besides, I don't even know if my abilities to burn up computers would work on a person!"

"And there's no point in trying to find out," Sean said. "Keira's right. We're going to do this the hard way, because that's the right way. We'll take the guy's toys away, but to expect her to become judge, jury, and…" He looked over at me, shaking his head. "…Executioner? No, that's not the way to do it." He nodded sharply. "I'm with her on this."

Devon sighed. "Okay, I guess. But it needed to be put on the table at least."

"Thanks, Sean," I said. Asshat that he was sometimes, he understood. He nodded again.

Devon turned to Gwen. "You haven't been to the house since you got back from Ireland."

"I know," she replied. "I've been busy with other stuff."

"Your mother's spirit would like to see you, hon. I get the sense from her that she's worried about you." Devon took a sip of water. "And on top of that, Buster hasn't seen you either."

Gwen ran a hand through her hair. "Yeah… I guess so. I don't know Dad, let me just do this mission with Keira, okay? As soon as it's done, I'll come back to the house; how's that?"

I shot a questioning look at Sean, who shrugged. This thing was taking its toll on everyone, that was for sure.

"What's the plan for tomorrow, dear?" Mom asked.

"I want to try doing it from so far away I can't see it. If I can pull that off, then we're going to have to work on the next step."

"Which is going to North Korea, right?" Dad said, with concern in his eyes. "How on earth do you plan on doing that? It's not like a trip to Florida, you know."

"One step at a time, Mr. Swanson," Sean said. He flashed a grin. "We'll jump off that bridge when we get to it."

What had to be the oddest dinner party I ever hosted broke up shortly afterward.

"I'll take you home, Pop," Sean said, rising from his seat. "I'll spend the night in my old room."

I felt a pang of disappointment and shot him a thought. *What, you no wanna fool around with me?*

He caught the thought and fired back. *With your parents under the same roof, I'd feel pretty damn weird about it. Can you blame me?*

Nooo… but you ever hear of a hotel?

He gave a slight shake of his head. *I think it'll be best if we keep our powder dry till this is all over, Keira.*

Damn. I knew I wasn't going to be able to budge him. I stuck out my tongue at him. *Asshat!*

He reached for me and took me in his arms and kissed me. Deeply, for real, and my knees went weak. I encircled my arms around his head with a 'MMmmmm' as I kissed him back. Then without warning, I pushed him away. "That's enough of that, or we'll be making a scene in the dining room!" Oh boy, could that guy get my motor running.

Devon laughed. "It's going to be some time before I can get that vision out of my mind!"

I immediately blushed.

"Let's get outta here, Pop," Sean said.

Seventeen

I'M NOT GOING TO LIE—I slept like a baby and woke up perfectly refreshed and ready to go with the next session bright and early. As I was coming downstairs to get some breakfast, the doorbell rang. I flung it open, grabbed Sean and kissed him deeply.

"Wow! Good morrrrning Keira!" he said, his eyes bright.

"Just think of what's in store *after* Korea," I said as I sashayed back inside toward the kitchen. I was wearing my hottest yoga pants, and knew he was enjoying the view.

We were all ready to go after breakfast. It was going to be the first time Mom and Dad were going to witness my newfound ability. I was a little rattled by them standing behind me, I'll admit it—I felt like a kid at a school recital. Because I was distracted, it took a little longer than last time.

Even so, I was able to fry another laptop, and this one was a football field length away, deep in a neighboring meadow!

Sean was a blip way down the property line but you couldn't miss him waving his hands high in the air when the laptop smoked and fell apart.

"That's amazing!" Dad said, stepping beside me. His mouth hung open. He shut it and turned to me. "I say we try a mile next."

"Shouldn't she rest before that?" Mom had come up to my other side, and her hand drifted across my back, rubbing it gently.

I sniffled, and there was a slight ringing in my ears as I settled down. Surprisingly, I didn't feel tired.

And that *awareness* had come back, even more intense than yesterday. The smoke from a diesel truck that was rambling down the highway a mile away; I knew that it had a weak U-joint, and I didn't even know what that was! I perked an ear hearing the chatter of chipmunks in the line of trees bordering the property; one had trespassed on another's territory! I stared at the field Sean was in, and felt the blades of grass emitting a gentle dark aura of energy.

Again, everything around me invaded all my senses.

A realization hit me. This was like tuning into the thoughts of people in crowded places. I needed to filter this to keep from going crazy. Yet, there was information in it which was important too.

This new sensitivity to the world could aid me!

I turned to my parents, "These nuclear weapons emit radiation don't they? Even before they blow up, they're giving some off, right?"

My mother surprised me by speaking first, "Yes. There's protective material on the outside but still considering what's inside, it can't get all of it. But the levels aren't so high that people can't be around them. You've seen news clips of servicemen working in missile silos, right? They weren't even wearing protective gear."

By this time Sean had arrived. *He* was wearing protective gear—a pair of oven mitts from the kitchen, and holding a misshapen hunk of plastic. It was still smoking.

"And another one bites the dust," Dad said.

Sean looked me up and down. "So, how're you feeling?"

"Fine! Ready to give it another go." I wanted to grab him, but I didn't want to while my ears were still ringing. I was worried he'd pick up on it and have a hissy fit.

"Hi everyone!" Gwen called, bounding across the yard to greet us. Her wavy, russet mane of hair bounced against her shoulders, while a flash of golden calves showed below her blue jean shorts. "How did it work at the greater distance?"

"Great! Keira's not even tired and it was almost five hundred feet." Dad's chin was high in the air, his chest puffed out like a rooster.

"Where's Roy?" Sean glanced at the house and then back at his sister. When they stood side by side, Gwen was only a few inches lower than his six-foot, athletic body. The same mop of curly hair but his eyes were ice blue while hers were gray.

"Dad phoned for a lift and Roy's taking Dad to his doctor's appointment."

"Not you?" Sean asked, watching her closely.

"Hell, no. I figured I'd be of more use here, silly." She wrapped an arm around my shoulders. "Keira and I usually do this psychic stuff side by side you know."

"Oh… well, that makes sense I guess." I noticed the twitch in his eyebrow. He was curious about Gwen avoiding their house too.

"Well," I said, "so far, so good for me. I nailed that one from way over in the Henderson field," I said pointing.

"Really? Awesome!"

I asked Gwen about radiation leaking from nuclear missiles, and she told me—albeit in more detail than I wanted to hear—all about gamma rays, and energized photons and yadda yadda until I held up my hand. "So do you think they would have their own aura?"

"Sure, I guess."

"Any idea how I could test it? To see what a radiation aura would look like?"

"Easy."

"Easy?"

"Sure! We'll just go to the hospital where they do CAT scans. Those suckers put out tons of ambient ergs, Keira. Not at dangerous levels, but you can give it a try there."

I didn't have a clue what an 'erg' was, and wasn't about to ask. I didn't need another ten-minute lecture of nuclear physics. I nodded. "Cool."

She turned to my folks. "When I talked with Dad on the phone he asked me to relay his thanks for a great dinner. It beat the frozen pizza he'd planned."

Mom's lower lip popped out. "Wow. A four-course roast beef dinner is better than a pizza from a freezer. Not sure if that's a compliment or not." She patted Gwen's arm and smiled. "We're going to try a mile this time. Want to go with me and the laptop? It's a Dell and I've got some issues with that company. I'd love to see it explode."

Gwen spun to look at Sean. "She's blowing them up now?"

"Just about." He held out my most recent victim. "The

screen shattered and fell off the base. She's getting stronger."

"Great. I can't wait to see this. I'll come with you, Susan." She picked up the Dell machine and jerked her head to my mother. "Let's head down the road a mile or so. My car's out front. I'll drive."

"Wait a second, I thought you were here for my backup," I said.

"You got my big brother looking after you; I'd like to see what happens at the other end." She turned and headed off with Mom.

"We'll call you when it's set up," Mom said.

Dad yelled to her, "Video it, will you?"

Mom turned and gave the thumbs-up signal before going in the sunroom door.

His hands were thrust deep in his pockets, and he looked over at Sean and me. "Would you like something to drink? A Coke or water? I need one."

"Sure. I'll take a bottle of water." I watched him walk to the house before turning to Sean and putting my arms around his neck. "That was nice of him to give us a few moments alone." I rose up on the tips of my toes to kiss his lips. A warm, slow, sensuous kiss that sent a thrill through me.

He grabbed the waistband of my yoga pants and yanked me over, so that we were snuggled closer. His hands caressed my back and cupped my butt, as he nuzzled my neck and ear. "You're doing this on purpose!"

I giggled. "Yuppers."

The door to the sunroom banged shut and then Dad appeared carrying a few bottles of water. "Your mother called. They're all set up and ready for you."

When he approached, I took the bottle and drained half of it. This was going to be hard. I couldn't see the target, yet I'd have to destroy it. This was more like what I'd face when we actually did this.

I handed the bottle to Sean and then stood, centering myself with deep breaths. When I felt the tingling start in my chest, my eyes closed. I pictured the laptop and guesstimated where it probably was set up. If only I could attain that level of consciousness that had followed the first couple of times I'd done this. I would be able to sense the exact location and pinpoint my focus.

The energy was building in my body but still the all-knowing awareness wasn't there. Minutes passed as I stood there, my body tense, my fists tight at my sides. Still nothing. I took a deep breath, my mind forcing a blast of energy in the direction I knew Gwen's house was. My body began to tremble with the effort. I knew I was close but not over the hump yet, not where I needed to be.

I turned to Sean and held my hand out. Immediately he stepped over. When he grasped it, the jolt of energy almost made me stumble to the side. Again, I faced the eastern direction and closed my eyes. This had to be enough. Where we touched seemed to spark, sending threads of energy up my arm and into my chest.

A fleeting glimmer of the laptop entered my mind and I pushed with all my might. My arm ached from the power, and a sharp pain almost split my temples in half.

Dad's cell phone ringing sounded like it was underwater. There, but barely audible.

There was only the laptop filling my mind, seeing the plastic sheath covering the components melting. I could smell the acrid stink of it, see the tendril of smoke swirling from the seams, hear the sizzle and pop of the metal inside.

Dad's voice was a low rumble from far away, like he was across the field. "It worked. You can stop, Keira."

But the power consumed me, made me one with the laptop and everything else—the trees bordering the property, my mother, her heartbeat fast as she gaped, a wasp buzzing near the veranda... It only stopped when I saw Gwen standing next to the seared, dark object, tossing a bucket of water onto it.

Sean's hand slipped from mine and I collapsed onto my knees. My heart was a racehorse pounding hard and fast. Oh God, the ringing in my ears was unbearable! I put my hands over them, rubbing briskly.

Sean dropped down beside me. "Hey..." His arm cradled me close, giving me the strength I needed. "You did it... you'll be okay..."

I turned to him and sighed. "No. *We* did it. I couldn't see it until you added your power to mine. I was close but not there." My head rose higher, and I stared at him, as if seeing him for the first time. There was a golden aura emanating from him that had never been there before.

"You're glowing, Sean." I held my hand up and my eyes opened wider, My fingertips also glowed where he'd touched me! When I looked down at my knees, the aura was a pale blue, threaded with white. Normally it was a rich blue, but silver? When we joined, it had changed.

"Oh yeah?" His head dipped lower, looking at himself. "Nope, I don't see anything."

"Take my word for it—it's there."

Dad was beaming, his smile barely visible from the hues of bright green enveloping him. "Your mother filmed everything. I can't wait to see it. This is amazing."

"I need a minute, guys." I closed my eyes, slowing my breathing to get control again. Normally auras were only visible when I unfocused my eyes. But now, the colors and impressions were overwhelming. My stomach rolled from the assault to my senses. Thankfully, the ringing in my ears stopped. I slid a finger in one and sneaked a peek at the tip.

Oh God.

There was blood on it. I huffed a sigh and wiped it on my black pants. I looked up at Sean. "How are you feeling?" I asked.

"Fine... no problem at all." I held out my hand and he pulled me to my feet.

"I'm okay now," I said. "But that was pretty wild." What had happened between us was power on steroids. I wasn't ready for that. But if we were to accomplish this, I'd have to be ready.

It was clear, that I couldn't do this without him. My shoulders fell and I sighed. It wasn't right. I needed to be able to do this on my own.

Didn't I?

Eighteen

WHEN GWEN AND MY MOTHER RETURNED with the laptop, they were both awed and excited.

"I've seen some strange stuff when I was a small girl with your Nana, Keira," Mom said. "But never..." She held up the wooden tray holding the still-smoking laptop. "Never anything like this!" She stared wide-eyed at it. "We set it on the ground and stepped away—"

"We went to the other side of the road, actually," Gwen interrupted. "We weren't sure of your aim!"

"Right!" Mom continued. "Nothing happened at first. Then it started to vibrate—"

"That must have been the buildup of energy you were sending it!" said Gwen. "That took an incredible amount of energy!" She looked at me carefully. "Are you feeling okay? I can't understand how your brain could do such a thing!"

Mom went still. "What do you mean, Gwen?"

"If you plug too many things into an extension cord, it gets warm, right? That's because it's trying to handle the energy going through." Gwen pointed at me. "What Keira just did was basically use her brain like a laser blaster!"

I waved my hand at her. "I don't know if it was my brain entirely," I said. "I think it had more to do with a connection to other, higher powers."

She pointed at me. "But you're the transmission line, Keira. Are you okay?" The concern in her voice was both touching and scary. Touching, because she was genuinely worried; her science background gave her a clue about how this could take a toll on me. But scary because I didn't want anyone to know how much a toll it was taking.

"I'm fine!" I said sharply. "Then what happened, Mom?"

Mom was watching the two of us, her mouth pinched. "Well..." She looked over at Gwen and tilted her head. "Gwen, just how much of a risk is this for Keira? Could this hurt her?"

"I'M FINE!" I shouted.

All of them jumped when I yelled. "Now what happened next?" I said in as calm a voice as I could.

Sean let out a sigh. "I think she's doing okay, Mrs. Swanson..."

But now Mom was giving me a 'Mom' look. She didn't pursue it, but I knew full well and clearly that this topic was far from over. She was going to bide her time before really coming down on me. Her lips pursed for a second and then she continued, "It started to shake really fast—vibrating... and then... and then..." She stared at me in silence.

Gwen picked it up. "Then it started to *glow*, Keira. Do you have any idea how much energy is needed to make plastic *glow*?"

I waved my hand. "Doesn't matter. Wasn't my energy; hell, I'm standing right here, fit as a fiddle!" Which was a lie. I could barely hear them over the ringing in my ears.

"Hmph," was all Mom said.

Gwen kept talking. "Next, the whole thing started smoking, and in a flash, flames burst from it for a couple of seconds, then everything stopped."

When she finished, I looked at all three of them, watching me like a hawk.

I threw up my hands. "Boo!" And they all jumped back, and I burst out laughing. "Gotcha!"

Sean shook his head. "You're a jerk."

But Mom's face eased, and that's all I cared about.

I started walking away toward the driveway where Gwen's car was the last in the lineup. "Gwen?" I said. "We need to go for a ride and do some research."

"What do you mean?"

I leaned over and spoke quietly. "I need to see if I can detect the aura of radioactive material." I waved at Mom and Sean as I hustled Gwen down the path. I called back to them, "We're just going into town for a little bit. You guys get lunch or something, okay?"

"Where to, boss?" she said as we got into the car.

"Because of Mom getting all worked up over your blabbing about energy I didn't want to say anything in front of her, but we're going to the hospital."

"Oh shit! You're hurt!"

I waved my hand at her. "No! I'm fine! I guess we're going to have to go to the hospital and check out the radiology department. They got radioactive material, and I need to see if I can detect its aura, that's all!"

"You sure you're okay?"

I was feeling better by the minute, so I just nodded. "I'm fine, hon. Now let's go."

We parked in the underground lot across the street from Kingston General Hospital. It's a fair-sized complex that's also a teaching hospital for the university that borders it. Located practically on the shore of Lake Ontario, half the place looks out over a blue expanse of water.

"It's this way," Gwen said, pointing the way. "We had to come here while Dad was being diagnosed for his multiple sclerosis. She headed down a rabbit warren of corridors until we arrived at the Radiology Department. "Okay, what now?"

We were in a waiting area which contained a row of chairs lined up along the wall. The clerk at a desk looked up at us. I nodded to her and said, "We don't have an appointment; I just need to sit here for a bit if that's okay."

She shrugged and went back to her work as Gwen and I sat down. I leaned over to Gwen and whispered, "I'm just going to sit here and see if I can sense the machine in the other room."

"Sure. Go for it."

I closed my eyes, centered myself, and reached out.

In my mind's eye, the walls and shielding around the CAT scanner became transparent, and I saw the enormous donut-shaped, steel-clad device. It was a huge tube, about the size of a cargo van, but round. There was a table at the front that slid up inside the machine, and a technician was behind a thick glass window doing some paperwork.

I flowed over the machine with my being, able to sense

its components. Every screw, electrical thingamajig, button and light were apparent to me. As I explored the device, I *understood* what each part was intended for! It was really strange—while I was immersed in it, I *understood* it. I marveled at how we humans could conceive and build such a device for healing. Turning my attention away from the gauges, power sources and all the other parts, I went a' hunting for the radioactive material.

It was easy to find. The radioactive material's aura was a sickly green, oozing with rivulets of yellow, like pus. I drew closer, examining it, and was able to detect tendrils of black worming through it.

Even though I knew this was being used in a medical device, this stuff was dangerous as hell.

I withdrew back into myself and gave Gwen a nudge. "I'm done here. Let's go find a dental office."

"What? Why?"

"They all have X-ray machines, right? They're radioactive or something, right?"

"Yeah."

"Okay then."

It didn't take long before we were pulled up before a dental practice in a shopping center.

"I'm going to do this from the car," I said. Once again, and it was easier this time, I launched away from myself and into the office. Now that I knew what I was looking for, I found it right away. Same disgusting color, but more muted because of the size of the pellet. I pushed my mind right up to its tiny form, caressing the surface of the radioactive pellet with my consciousness. I pushed against it and knew I'd be able to screw it up with no problem. Good.

My head jerked on the car's headrest when I returned to

myself. I turned to Gwen. "I did some reading online about nuclear warheads," I said. "They're made of two different pieces that get slammed together, right?"

She shrugged. "Yeah. I don't know a lot about them, I was more interested in other things in physics, but we talked about them when I was an undergrad. They're machined to pretty stringent tolerances—within a hundred thousandth of an inch."

"So if I could mess up their shape just a little, they won't work?"

She nodded. "Pretty much. They'd get hot, start melting on their own, but no, they wouldn't blow up."

"Good." A plan was starting to form in my head. "Let's head home."

I talked with her about it on the run back to the house, and Gwen thought it could work. When we pulled into the driveway of my house I saw a rental car parked outside that gave me one bad feeling. I hustled into the house, and stopped dead at the entrance to the living room.

"You got some damn nerve coming here, bitch!" I hissed through clenched teeth at Cora Gaines. Sitting way too damn close to Sean on the couch!

Nineteen

H ELLO, KEIRA."

Even her voice was repugnant. No forewarning, no phone call, just there. Her hair was swept up in the familiar French knot, nothing out of place, with more than a few silvery threads extending from her temples. The lines of crow's feet bordered the outer corners of chocolate-colored eyes although in the short time I'd been with her, I'd never seen her laugh or even manage a grin. She looked every bit mid-forties on the downward slide to matronly. I don't care if I sound catty; it's the truth.

And if she was here hoping to rekindle any romance with Sean, she sure hadn't dressed the part in the gray pantsuit my *mother's* generation wouldn't wear.

"What the hell makes you think you can walk into *my*

house!" I stormed across the room and stood before her.

"Hey, hey—take it easy," Sean said, holding up a hand. "I contacted her and asked her to come!"

I looked over at him, furious. "What? Without so much as telling me? *Asking* me if it was okay?"

Sean leapt to his feet. "Now look!" He pointed at Cora. "She's got contacts all around the world through the Illuminata! If anyone could help us get as close to those missiles, it would be her!"

Cora's voice was smooth as silk, totally unruffled by my outburst. She sat perched on the edge of the couch and added, "Unless, of course, you have a plan already in place to take care of those." She coughed an 'ahem.' "*Minor* details."

I opened, then closed my mouth. I had nothing. "I only just figured out how I can actually do this, Cora. I'll figure those *details* out now."

"I'm sure." She made a small shrug with her shoulders. "As we speak, the Illuminata are marshaling our resources and contacts in both South *and* North Korea to provide you with assistance." She leaned forward. "Tell me Keira, have you ever been to the Koreas?" She made a small smile. "Could you even find them on a map?"

Shit. I knew they were in Asia someplace. I decided to change tack. "How is Esther?"

"She's well. She's settled in, although she's exhibiting some behavioral problems." Cora shook her head sadly. "That girl has a temper!"

"I'll bet. You screwed her out of her chance for a happy life, bitch!"

Cora jumped to her feet and got right in my face. "I'm giving her a chance *at* life, you fool! What do you think is going to happen when you fail?" She held out her arms. "All this around you is going to become a wasteland! Where she is, Esther will be able to survive and thrive and pick up the pieces after you fools!"

"Hey, hey, let's everybody take a breath," Sean said quietly, getting between the two of us. Which was a good idea, because I was about to sock her one. He looked at me. "Don't even think of it, Keira," he said.

I gritted my teeth.

"So this is the famous Cora Gaines?" Gwen said, her arms crossed. She looked from Cora to Sean. "And you had a thing with this woman, Sean? She's practically as old as Dad!"

I smiled, watching Cora's face turn red.

"It's not like that," Sean said. But the look of hurt in Cora's eyes said he wasn't being completely honest.

"I take it you're Gwendolyn," Cora said. "I've heard a lot about you." She held out her hand to shake Gwen's.

Gwen scoffed and took a step back holding her hands up. "I wouldn't touch you with a ten-foot pole, granny."

Whoa. Even I was surprised at how damn *harsh* she was being.

Cora dropped her hand and tilted her head at Gwen. "I see." She turned to Sean. "As I was explaining to Sean, time is running out. We're going to need to take action immediately."

I blanched. "Immediately? What the hell are you talking about? We just got started!"

She looked at the three of us. "Have any of you so much as looked at the news lately?" When she saw the blank look on our faces, she sighed. You have a television?"

"Yeah," I pointed to a bookcase. "I don't watch it much,

but it's in that cabinet."

"Turn it on to a news channel."

I stepped over and opened the doors and grabbed the remote and flicked it on. I pressed some buttons.

There was a live feed from in front of The Capitol building where Dad and I met with Uncle Bob just a couple of days ago. People were streaming out of it carrying boxes of papers.

"Well, Wolfe, while this looks like a scene of a mass layoff at a Wall Street brokerage, it's anything but. Since the aircraft carrier Nimitz exploded and sunk yesterday in the South China Sea, Congress has declared an unscheduled recess, and all of the members of both the House and Senate are returning home to their constituencies. While the government has not made any formal declaration of a state of emergency, all of these Congressional staffers obviously know something the public does not."

"What's that, Anderson?" a voiceover asked.

The camera panned back to the correspondent on the scene. "Washington D.C. is being evacuated."

Gwen, Sean, and I stared dumbfounded at the TV screen.

Cora clicked off the set and turned to us. "We have to act quickly," she said.

I looked around the house. "Where are my parents?"

"Where's my dad?" Gwen said.

"They're upstairs packing," Sean said to me. He turned to Gwen. "Dad's at home grabbing some things too."

"Why?"

Cora spoke. "Arrangements have been made for them to wait this out in Norway." She looked over at Gwen. "And I had to pull some serious strings in order to accommodate your father's dog, I might add."

"Don't expect my thanks, dear," she replied. "You did it for Sean, not for me."

"You still benefit, *dear*."

Good grief, this woman was as catty as... well, me, I guess.

I ran up the stairs.

Mom had the trunk of mementos opened, and was pulling things from it and making two piles. She looked up, her face tear streaked. "I... we... can only bring one suitcase each..." she said. "I packed some underwear and a pair of pants..." She gestured at the pile of photos, scrapbooks, and memories littering the bed. "I've already taken your school pictures, and..." She put her hands over her face. "Our wedding photooooos." Her voice ended in a sob.

Dad had a suitcase loaded and dropped what he had. "Susan! Get hold of yourself!" He stepped over to her and took her in his arms. "You do the best you can, honey, but you're not doing Keira any favors by breaking down!"

She leaned into him and let out a howl of pain. "So many people are going to diiiie!" She wailed. "Mrs. Bernstien next door to us! The crew at the coffee shop! They're all going to diiie! And their mothers! And fathers! And, and all the chillldreeen!" She clutched at him. "There were over five thousand sailors on that boat that blew up, Richard! They were all so young! Five thousand kids! Like that! Gone!"

I stood there helpless, watching Mom's heart break. Dad held her to his chest, stroking her back. "I know, baby, I know..."

I started to cry myself, and stepped into them. Our arms encircled each other, grasping and holding one another tightly. Even Dad was getting misty.

"Susan, we all gotta be as strong as we can for the next while, hon. This isn't going away, and we'll have to face this."

"Don't go, Keira! Come with us to Norway!" Mom said. She clutched at me, pulling me into her. "I couldn't go on if anything happened to you!" I let her hold on to me, and rubbed her back as she continued her meltdown.

I have never, not once in my life, seen my mother in such straits. More than demons, or nuclear war, or any ghosty shit I had encountered; seeing my mother fall apart scared the hell out of me.

"Oh *mommy*..." I said, holding her.

We all turned at the rapping on the doorjamb. Cora was standing there. "We need to leave," she said. "Now."

"I'm not finished packing!" Mom said, breaking away from Dad and I.

"Mrs. Swanson!" Cora said sharply. She shot a look at me. "Believe it or not, the world does *not* revolve around you and your family!" She stepped over to the bed beside Mom and began flinging photo albums and envelopes into her suitcase. "Your flight is a feeder flight. It's going to be landing in less than thirty minutes, and taking off immediately afterward. We have a trans-Atlantic flight prepared in Ottawa with an extremely narrow time window!" She bustled the suitcase closed, picked it up and strode to the bedroom door. "We need to leave *now*."

"C'mon, honey," Dad said. "The quicker this is done, the easier it will be to deal with." He put his arm around Mom and we all followed Cora downstairs.

Roy was out front with the Escalade. I saw Devon was already on board, with Gwen and Roy standing beside it.

When we reached the car, Roy loaded their bags while

Mom held my shoulders. "We're saying goodbye here, Keira," she said.

"But—"

She shushed me. "No. Your father's right. This isn't easy, and you've got bigger fish to fry than a trip to the airport." She looked over at Cora, standing there nodding.

"That's a good idea, Mrs. Swanson," Gwen said. "Roy and I have already said our goodbyes to Dad. Sean and…" She jerked a thumb at Cora. "This woman will take you guys to the flight."

"I have to line up transportation to Asia," Roy said. "It's not going to be easy; charters are being snapped up like crazy since the news about that aircraft carrier broke. Everyone who is able to is getting out of the States as fast as they can."

Cora looked at us. "Very well. Sean and I will be back as soon as we can." She got into the shotgun seat next to Sean, and I said goodbye to my parents.

As the vehicle headed down the driveway and turned onto the road toward the airport I asked Gwen, "Do you think we'll ever see them again?"

She didn't say anything.

Twenty

I HATE THAT BITCH," GWEN SAID. Her fingers curled into fists at her side.

"Hey babe," Roy sidled up next to her and put his arm around her waist. "That's pretty harsh talk about the woman who's saving your dad's life and even Buster's, you know."

She plucked his hand from her. "I don't really care for that dog." Her eyes were still watching the driveway, even though they had been gone for a few moments. "Pets are overrated, don't you agree, Keira?" she added, turning toward me.

I snorted. "I don't know... I always wanted a dog. But all my life, dogs have been afraid of me." It's true. For as long as I can remember, anytime I'd meet a dog, tiny lap dogs all the way up to German shepherds; pit bulls and poodles... didn't matter. They'd take one look at me, tuck their tails and do everything they could to get as far away from me as possible. When I met Gwen, her dog Buster, a friendly, loping, loving mutt, took off at the first sight of me, and always made himself scarce whenever I would go to her father's home down the road.

"See?" Gwen sniffed. "Well, you're not missing anything. Dumb animals." She pointed to the end of the driveway. "Enough of that. If I never lay eyes on that bitch again, I'll be fine."

I shot a look at Roy, who looked just as puzzled as I felt. I looked at Gwen from the corner of my eye to see her aura was pulsing purple and red. It looked oddly familiar, but I couldn't place it. "Well, I have no love for her either," I said. "But your brother sure thinks highly of her."

"He's a fool!"

"Whoa!" I had never seen Gwen so vehement. "Look Gwen, we're going to have to work with her. What she said about having contacts in Korea is true." I shook my head. "I *think* I might be able to do something to those missiles, but Cora's done a lot of homework on this. We're going to have to work with her."

"Hmph," she snorted. "Over my dead body."

"Gwen!" Roy said. "What the hell's gotten into you? I've never seen you react to someone like this!"

She tilted her head back, looking down her nose at him. Roy was about two inches shorter than Gwen. "You watch yourself, Roy. I hate Cora, and that should be enough for you."

"Watch myself?" His face flared red and he stepped up to her. "What the hell's going on here? You threatening me? Me?" I saw his hands clench.

Holy shit. The mood was downright *toxic* right now! I don't know what the hell just happened, but Gwen had gone from being bitchy to venomous! And to Roy of all people! "Hey!" I barked. "Take it easy!" They both turned to me.

Gwen spat out, "I'm taking your side, you idiot!"

And out of nowhere, a fury rose up in me. I felt it boil up from my stomach and shoot through my head. "Oh yeah?" I said. Okay, not my best repartee, but I went from puzzled to pissed in a split second.

"Damn right!" she hissed. "That Cora bitch is screwing around with us, and I'm standing up for *you*!" She gestured at Roy. "If he wants to be an asshole, fine!"

Roy's face looked like he was just slapped. His head rocked back from her invective and snapped forward again. He stared at me, then at Gwen. He turned around without saying a word and went back into the house.

"Fine!" she called after him.

I reached out and grabbed her by the upper arms. I gave her a hard shake. "What the hell's the matter with you?"

In a split second, her face became a mask of rage, her lips pulled back, baring her teeth. The next second she went completely still and blinked at me a couple of times. She looked back to the house, and then to me. "Ohhh Keira..." she said and covered her face with her hands. "It's so hard..."

"Hey, hey..." Just as I had done with my mother, I put my arms around her. Sometimes, when the world is falling apart, all you can do, and the best you should do, is hold on tight to someone you love.

I held my weeping best friend with all my might.

Then all hell broke loose.

Twenty One

M Y HEAD WHIPPED UP at the sound of tires screeching at the end of my driveway. A huge, black four by four came roaring up, spewing a rooster tail of gravel and dust.

Gwen and I stood there in shock, still embraced as it crunched to a halt in front of us. I could see two men in black suits behind the windshield.

"Oh shit," I said. It was Brandon and Brandon.

They smiled brightly, and as if choreographed, popped open their doors and stepped out of the vehicle, the engine still running.

"Good day, Ms. Swanson!" Brandon said, cheerfully as they stepped together at the front of the SUV and walked toward us. "And this must be Gwen Jones, I assume!" The other Brandon looked at the house where Roy had launched through the door and was running down the steps toward us. "And Roy as well! As I live and breathe!"

"Who... who are you?" Gwen said as Roy pulled up beside us.

I pointed a finger. "That's Brandon," I said. I pointed at the second man. "And that too, is Brandon." They both made slight bows, keeping their eyes on us. "What do you want?"

"To protect our nation," the first one said.

"By securing it from enemies, foreign and domestic of course!" said the other.

"Who are you with?" Roy asked.

They both looked at him, as if their heads were attached on a string. "Why, the government, Roy!" Brandon said.

"Oh yeah? Let me see your identification," Roy said.

"We prefer to just keep this encounter casual," one of the Brandons said.

"Casual?" I said. "You guys just pulled in here like you were auditioning for the latest *Mission Impossible* movie!" The cloud of dust they kicked up was only now clearing.

"Pretty impressive, don't you think?" the Brandon who had been driving said. He jerked his thumb at his partner. "Brandon wanted us to come to a slewing stop straight out of *The Fast and the Furious*, but I thought that would have been overdoing it." He held his hands out, palms up. "At any rate, we meet again, Keira!"

"IDs, please," Roy said, holding out his hand.

Brandon ignored him and stepped up to me. "We're here on orders from the highest levels, Keira."

"Oh?" The lighthearted casualness of these two was the most menacing thing about them. "And what would those orders be?"

He shrugged slightly. "A simple issue of having you…" He pointed to Gwen, then Roy. "And you and you surrender your passports, so you can remain in Canada and not pose a threat."

"Surrender our passports?"

"Yes. We have acquired information that you're planning on visiting Korea very soon."

"Where'd you hear that?"

"You intend to involve yourself in the crises currently underway between the United States and North Korea." He shook his head slowly. "And that just *won't do*."

"You plan on stopping me?"

"You don't belong there. So, our choice…" He looked to his partner who nodded. "Is to ensure that you remain here in Canada… or take all of you into custody."

The other Brandon spoke up. "And our custody will not be nearly as comfortable as the accommodations in Norway your families are heading to."

"That's true," first Brandon said. "However, your brother Roy, Gwen, along with a Ms. Gaines is right now experiencing our humble hospitality as we speak!"

"You have Sean?" I gasped.

"Only for the duration of this crises; don't worry." He looked at Roy. "Mr. Sean Jones disputed our authority and together with Ms. Gaines declined to voluntarily cooperate."

"What did you do to them!" I said.

He held up his hand. "One thing at a time, Keira." He held his hand out. "Your passports, please."

"Screw you, bubba!" Roy said. He stepped between Brandon and I and shoved with his chest.

Brandon didn't move, and Roy bounced off with a look

of surprise. Brandon held up a warning finger. "Don't. Do. That. Again," he said, his voice no longer cheerful. He turned back to me. "You'll either surrender your passports, or we'll confiscate them. And if we have to confiscate them, we'll search for them. And we won't be tidy about it."

"It's a big house, Brandon; you'll be here all day."

He shook his head slowly. "No, I think we'd be done quickly. Not neatly, but quickly, yes." He gestured to my home behind me, three stories of a Victorian manor. "We'd have that place reduced to a pile of sticks in about an hour or so."

I looked from Brandon to Brandon. "I don't think so."

"I see." He nodded to his partner.

The other Brandon lifted his arm and spoke into his sleeve. "Prepare for insertion!" he barked. He looked back to Brandon. "Fifteen seconds out."

The other Brandon looked at his watch. "Excellent."

"What the hell's going on?" I said.

Brandon held up his hand in a shushing gesture.

In the next second, the air around us was filled with a roar. From behind the trees that lined the shores of Lake Ontario opposite my home, four huge helicopters popped up. My jaw dropped as they came over the house and hovered. Huge doors on the side slid open and from each aircraft about a dozen coils of rope dropped down, reaching the grounds of my home.

"There are forty-eight operatives inside those helicopters, Keira!" Brandon yelled over the roar of the engines. "They'll have your home *dismantled* in no time, and we will have your passports! Furthermore, if their feet touch the ground, all of you *will* be taken into custody!"

I stared up at the helicopters. "Wait here!" I ran into the

house and grabbed my purse. Since I started doing my work with The Veil, Gwen, Roy and I all kept our passports within arm's reach. I ran back down to the driveway, digging away.

"Give them your passports guys," I said. I dug out my own and handed it to Brandon. Roy pulled his out of his back pocket, and Gwen fished hers from her purse.

One of the Brandons raised his arms in the air making an 'X' with them. He then drew his hand across his throat.

As fast as they had dropped, the ropes were spun back up inside the helicopters. The doors slid closed, and in formation, they turned and went back over the tree line and disappeared.

The silence, after the roaring noise was compelling on its own.

I gaped at the two of them. "Where did they come from? Where are they going?"

"They have a short jaunt back over the border to the States. There's a military base just thirty-five miles away as the chopper flies. It's called Fort Drum, and there is a staging base there for…" He smiled like a shark, "For *highly skilled* and exceptionally trained soldiers."

"But this is Canada! You can't *do* that!" Roy said.

"They didn't do anything, did they? And there's no record of them ever being here." He tapped the passports into line against his palm and smiled again. "Thank you for your cooperation. We'll be watching."

With a nod to his partner, they returned to their SUV and left.

The three of us stared after them, then at one another.

"Now what do we do?" Gwen asked.

Twenty Two

I LOOKED AT THEM BOTH. "We go dark," I said and headed to the house.

"What the hell does that mean?" Gwen said after me as she and Roy followed.

I went through the front door and to the right where the library was. When I first came to Kingston, that room had been Nana's sick room. Since she passed, I had the hospital bed removed and restored the room to its original state. I went to one of the bookcases, slid my hand under one of the shelves and pressed a button.

A spring latch behind the bookcase released, and it popped about three inches from the wall. I tugged on it, but it was too heavy. "Give me a hand, will you guys?" They stepped over, and the three of us pulled the bookcase from the wall. It was on a hidden hinge, and opened into a small room.

There were a series of switches on the doorjamb and I flipped them.

The small windowless room was bathed in light. It wasn't much bigger than a walk-in closet. There was a row of old-fashioned, wooden file cabinets lining the back of it, a small writing desk and an ancient, wooden swivel chair tucked against the wall.

"Holy James Bond," Roy said.

"What the hell is this?" Gwen's voice had an edge of surprise in it.

"Nana had this constructed as soon as she bought the place," I said. "She initially had it built as a panic room in case David Holmes ever got up to something and came here. I nodded to a steel cabinet. "Lawrence had that put in—there's some old guns in there he locked up until they passed on." I stepped over to one of the file cabinets. "She kept handwritten notes and records of every incident she had with The Veil." My eyes began to tear up. "She made me start writing notes the third day I was here of everything we ever did together…" My voice cracked as I tapped the top drawer. It had a label on the front that said 'Keira.' "And, since you and I started doing this Gwen, I've been keeping up on the records."

Gwen's eyes narrowed. "Why didn't you tell me about this room?" There was an edge to her voice.

"Well, first of all, because Nana told me to keep its existence a secret. I haven't even told *my parents* about it, Gwen."

"They don't work with you, Keira. I do."

Yeah, she was definitely annoyed. Which bugged me. "Hang on a second. I'm not obligated to tell you everything, you know. You work *for* me."

"Oh? *For* you? Not *with* you, huh?"

"Hey, hey, hey!" Roy said sharply. He looked at each of us. "Keira's telling us now because she thinks this is the right time, Gwen." He looked at me. "But you've got to admit, it makes one wonder what else you've not told us about, Keira. I mean, we do some really weird shit, and this room..." He waved his arm. "Says that you're keeping stuff back from us." He gestured at the cabinets. Each drawer had a label with a date range on it. Nineteen sixty-eight to seventy-five, nineteen seventy-five to eighty-three, and so on. "Those files have to do with The Veil and our work. Don't you think we should have the opportunity to read them?"

"No," I said firmly. "Because they're not just notes about her different exploits, Roy... She has a lot of really personal stuff in there too. It's like her diary. When Nana told me about these files, she made me promise not to go into them until she was gone."

I didn't realize at the time just how soon that was going to be.

Gwen crossed her arms. "Well, I think we should have access to them."

I waved my hand briskly. "We'll discuss that after we save the world, okay?" I went to the last cabinet in the row and pulled out the bottom drawer. The label there read, 'Special Documents.' "I came here for this," I said, and lifted out a metal strongbox from the drawer.

"What's in that?"

"Cover." I said. I opened the box. I pulled out several stacks of U.S. currency. Each one had a band around it that was marked two thousand dollars. I piled a few rows of ten bundles on the table. "That's about eighty thousand in cash, just in case," I said. "We'll probably need ready cash where we're heading."

"And just where is that?" Roy asked.

"Korea, of course."

"How the hell are we going to get into Korea when we don't have passports?"

"We do." I fished around in the box and pulled out three bundles. I kept one and gave them each one. "These are phony IDs. Driver's license, a couple of credit cards, a gym membership for you, Gwen, and a pilot's license for you, Roy." They took them silently and started riffling through them.

"Gwen Jones, you're now Ginny James. Roy Clark, you're now Ray Clerk."

"You made up phony IDs for us?" Roy said in astonishment.

I nodded. "We have to get on a plane to South Korea, Roy. And you can't do that. It's too long a flight for a single pilot."

"What's your new name?" Gwen asked.

I fingered my bundle of documentation and blinked back some tears. "Pamela York," I said.

"That's your grandmother's name!" Gwen said.

"I know, I know. It took some arm twisting of the guy who made these, but I insisted."

"Yeah! Who did that?" Roy asked.

"Never mind," I said with a wave of my hand. "We've got to get to South Korea. Let's get moving."

Four hours later we were at the ticket counter of Korea Air Lines at the Toronto Airport. There was no lineup at all. We each purchased our tickets, and paid for them with the credit cards I had doled out earlier. If something was going to go wrong, better to find out now than when we landed.

The tickets were approved, and we headed to the gate. As we headed down the concourse, I saw the departure board for this terminal. Flight after flight to Asia—Japan, Seoul, Beijing were being canceled.

"Good thing we came when we did," Roy said. "This flight is one of the last ones heading there for the next few days. That's what the clerk at the counter told me. All the airlines are bringing every plane they can out of the region and stopping service until things calm down."

"Really?" Gwen asked.

He snorted. "At a hundred million dollars and up for a commercial jet... yeah, they're going to look after them." He tilted his head and said in a thoughtful voice. "I'll bet their insurance companies demanded it."

The realization that huge companies were that worried about the world blowing up and did something as stupid as finding new parking spots for their planes instead of screaming bloody murder sent a chill through me. I chided myself. We were working to save the world, not change it.

Twenty Three

THE FLIGHT WAS ALMOST VACANT. In the first class section there were only a few other passengers, and the back of the plane was just as thinly populated.

"Well," Roy said, glancing around the cabin. With a weak smile, "Well, look at the bright side. There won't be a big lineup at customs when we arrive." He and Gwen took two seats that were next to one another in the center of the cabin, and I took the single by the window.

I had a thought. "Now that I think of it, what time will it be when we arrive, Roy? I mean, International Date Line and everything like that gets me mixed up."

"You're not the only one," he said. He looked at his watch. "Let's see... we're scheduled wheels up at six oh five, then it's just over fourteen hours in the air, and we'll be fighting headwinds… call it fourteen and a half. He stared off into space. "Fourteen hours flight time… time zone changes… uhhh…"

Gwen shook her head and snickered. "Come on, Roy! It's simple math!" She turned to me. "We'll arrive in Seoul at ten forty-five p.m. tomorrow night!"

My mouth dropped. "You figured all that out in your head? Just like that? Holy shit, you *are* a genius!"

She shrugged. "Yeah, my grad degree in physics really prepared me…" She held up her boarding pass. "To read my plane ticket! It's right on it silly!"

"Oh." I shot a look at Roy.

"Hey!" he said, holding up his hand. "I'm usually behind the wheel on these things! I can't remember the last time I bought a plane ticket!"

"Well, it's gonna be a long night," I said. It was going to be darkness our entire flight. I'd probably sleep most of the way.

As if. I could never sleep on a plane, and with what was waiting for us at the other end, well…

A few hours into the flight, Roy and Gwen were out cold under a blanket. I tried to read, watch a movie, and even sleep; nothing worked. I got out of my seat to at least stretch my legs and headed to the lavatory.

A high-pitched, muffled sob coming from the flight-crew galley section grabbed my attention. I heard another voice offering comforting words, but the keening continued.

I pulled the curtain separating the area from the cabin and stuck my head in.

Two flight attendants huddled in the far corner, facing away, looking out a porthole. One was young, about my age, and an older woman, wearing a blazer over her uniform held her shoulder shushing her. They were speaking in hurried hushed tones in Korean, and I couldn't understand the language.

"Excuse me..." I said.

The older woman looked up. "I'm sorry, but this area is for crew only, miss," she said in a tone that was used to being listened to. I couldn't help but think I was dealing with an Asian version of Cora Gaines.

"I know," I said, stepping over to them. "Is there anything I can do to help?"

The younger girl's head snapped up, and she spat out a stream of Korean that sounded vicious. The older woman's eyes flew open wide in shock, but spoke gently to the young girl.

The human heart speaks a universal tongue. I reached out with my mind.

"Soo-jin, this woman has nothing to do with it," the supervisor, Mrs. Lee, I learned, had said.

"Damn her, and all those asshole Americans! Our country is going to burn because of them, and this yellow-haired bitch will go to Disney World!" Soo-jin spat out, her eyes fiery as she looked from Mrs. Lee to me. *"She and her oh-so-great country just started a war!"*

"She did nothing, child. Nothing. She's blameless in all this..." The woman stroked the side of the girl's head. *"We'll be home soon enough, and you will know for sure about your brother."*

"What happened, Mrs. Lee?" I asked.

She looked at me, a little perplexed for a moment. With a sigh, she said in English, "There was a battle in the Yellow Sea, not far from Seoul. Ships and planes from American and our country's forces fought the North Koreans. Many dead..."

"Including my brother!" Soo-jin spat out in English. "He pilot for Republic Air Force! Thirty of our planes shot down!" She burst into tears, and fisted her eyes. "He dead! I know he dead!" Her voice was a venomous hiss.

It wasn't hard to learn his name when I probed. "Shit! He's your twin, Soo-jin!" I said before I could stop myself.

Mrs. Lee's face turned stony. "You spy? You work for CIA? How you know that?"

"No, I'm not a spy," I said, shaking my head. "I have..." I looked at them both. "Gifts."

"Gifts?"

"Yes." I looked next to the women. There was a folding-down jump seat that the crew would strap themselves into during landings. It was big enough to hold two people. I reached over, undid the latch and lowered the seat. The women stared at me dumbfounded as I sat on it.

"You can't—" Mrs. Lee started to say before I cut her off with a wave of my hand.

"Sit with me, Soo-jin," I said aloud. I sent a thought to her mind, and included Mrs. Lee. *Let's go find Min-Soo.* I held my hand out. *Hold my hand and close your eyes.*

She did as I asked, and as soon as I closed my eyes, we shot into the Astral Plane.

I heard her gasp. *Fear not.* I sent the thought to her, and she relaxed a little.

Like a bolt of lightning on steroids, our minds shot out of the side of the airliner, through the skies, across the black ocean below, over the Korean peninsula to the Yellow Sea.

Pure grief and fear burst in my mind from Soo-jin. *He down there!* she exclaimed. *He hurt!*

We shot across the water's surface to the side of a

hulking, gray naval warship. We went through the steel hull as easily as passing though a foggy mist and were at the ship's hospital.

Moans, of wounded sailors and pilots, filled the air as doctors, nurses and attendants worked through the broken and wounded young men. Against one of the walls was a stack of figures covered with a stained sheet—the ones that were pulled from the water but didn't make it. Scraps of fabric, remnants of uniforms cut from the wounded littered the floor.

Doctors snapped commands to their assistants, their tones razor sharp. The ward was bedlam busy, but these people were in control.

At the end of one row of gurneys, two attendants in scrubs wrapped a cast over the leg of an unconscious patient.

Min! Soo-jin's mind cried out in grief. *Min!*

The guy's eyes fluttered open and he stared off. "Jin...?" His voice was hazy, probably from painkillers. *Broke my damn leg punching out, sis...*

I thought you were dead!

Min smiled. "Not me, sis..." he said aloud. Dropping his head, he closed his eyes and fell back asleep.

A wave of exhaustion flowed over me. Everything that had been sharp and clear was beginning to fade black at the edges. *We need to go back.*

With a 'pop' I let go of her hand, and we were back inside the plane.

Soo-jin leapt to her feet and embraced Mrs. Lee. *Min's okay! He's hurt, but he's on a ship! He broke his leg but they rescued him!* she rattled off in Korean.

Mrs. Lee held her, and watched me. "Who are you?" she

said. "How did you do this?"

"I told you, I have gifts…" I said. "I need to get back to my seat now, I think…" I tried to stand, but when I pushed myself out of the seat, my legs gave way.

They grabbed me, and helped me back to the cabin. Soo-jin fussed over me, saying over and over in English and Korean how grateful she was. I nodded dumbly. I just needed to sleep.

Mrs. Lee came back and shooed Soo-jin away. She pressed a button on the side of my chair and it reclined into a small bed. "You sleep now, Miss Pamela," she said in a gentle voice. "You not a spy…"

I shook my head with the cobwebs. Pamela? Why was she—then it hit me, I was traveling under an alias. "I tried to tell you that," I said, my voice sleepy.

"You no spy. You an angel."

I snorted. Not with the sinful thoughts of Sean Jones I've been having!

Twenty Four

SOO-JIN NUDGED ME AWAKE. "We're on final approach, Miss Pamela. You need to set your chair back up for landing," she whispered to me. Her eyes were still wide in awe from what we had done.

"Thank you," I said as I fumbled at the buttons bringing my seat back up to normal.

I probed her mind. She wanted to ask me if the war was really going to happen, but was restraining herself. She was still in awe of the miracle with her twin brother... but there was more to it that was holding her back.

She was afraid of me.

Feeling her sense of fear... of *me* was deflating. But I had to admit to myself that as much as that realization stung, how could I blame her? I had taken her by the hand and completely screwed with her mind like a bad trip on LSD. Sure it only lasted a few minutes, but it was going to take Soo-jin a long, long time to process it. I smiled at her wistfully, and she returned to the front of the cabin.

Gwen and Roy had also been roused, and were sitting up.

"How was your flight?" I asked, leaning forward from my seat.

"Too long," Gwen grumped. "I feel like shit."

Roy was still blinking owlishly. "Saving the world's a real pain in the ass, you know. Playing tour guide to ghosts is a hell of a lot easier." He shook off some more cobwebs and looked at me. "Just what are we going to do when we land?"

"Don't worry about that," I said lightly. "I got this." I sat back into my seat, closing my eyes and cutting off the conversation.

I didn't have the slightest idea what we were going to do.

It wasn't long after, with our luggage in tow we stood at a deserted taxi stand. Instead of the typical lineup of cabs, the boulevard in front of the terminal was deserted.

"This is strange," Gwen said, her mouth a frown. "It's a ghost town here."

Roy came out of the automatic doors. "Even the car rental desks are closed," he said.

"Damn it!" Gwen spat. "We should have gone to Norway with the others! Instead…" She spread her arms. "We're stranded in an airport, in a country where we don't speak the language—hell, we don't even have the same alphabet—just in time for a war to break out!"

I was beyond beat; all I wanted to do was get to a hotel and sleep for a week. The Astral Travelling I did with Soo-jin took more out of me than I expected. "Look Gwen, we'll figure out how to get to a hotel, get some sleep and try to figure something out in the morning, okay?"

"Oh yeah? How? How are we going to get to a hotel,

huh? I'll bet even the busses aren't running either!"

Before I could think of an answer that I really didn't have, a sub-compact car pulled up to the curb beside us.

"How'd you do that, Keira?" Roy said.

"I..." Before I could say anything else, the driver's door opened and a woman got out. It was Mrs. Lee from our flight. I stared at her dumbly.

"I was afraid you might be here," she said. "I had hoped you had made arrangements to be picked up, but came by just to make sure."

"Well, our plans were pretty last minute," I said.

"I can drive you wherever it is that you're going, Miss Pamela," she said.

"We just need to get to a hotel, so I can get some sleep," Gwen said.

I shot her a look. I was completely dead on my feet, and she's saying that *she* was tired? "You guys slept practically the entire flight!" I said.

"Yeah, I'm feeling pretty good," Roy said.

"I just want to get the hell out of here!" Gwen snapped.

"Okay, okay!" We loaded our bags into the trunk of Mrs. Lee's car and got in.

"Where to?" she asked.

"The closest five star hotel in this town," Gwen said from the backseat.

I refrained from biting her head off.

"Very well," Mrs. Lee said, putting the car in gear. "I'll take you to the Westin Chosun. It's in the heart of the city and is one of the best hotels in the city."

Gwen folded her arms with a huff. "As long as people speak English, and the sheets are clean, I'm good."

I spun around to bite her head off, but Mrs. Lee put a

hand on my arm and shook her head. "You're friend is tired," she said. "Many times, such a long flight makes people's tempers fray."

I relaxed in the passenger seat beside her as she navigated through the city. "Well," I said, "we're under some pressure."

Mrs. Lee looked out at the vacant streets as we glided through the city. There was practically no traffic at all. "I understand. My entire country is under considerable pressure."

"What's going on here?" I asked.

"I just found out when we landed. The government has declared martial law. That hasn't happened since nineteen fifty when we were at war with North Korea."

"That's a big deal. Why?"

"Because they also declared full mobilization, and are worried about unrest." She pointed out the window. "That's why the streets are so deserted." She pressed her lips together. "Every able-bodied man and woman between the ages of eighteen and thirty-five is being called up to the military."

Gwen spoke from the backseat. "Well, I hope this Westin Hotel is still open!"

"Don't worry," Mrs. Lee responded. "My husband works there. They're taking in guests. I phoned him as soon as we landed to see how he is. He's at work." She shrugged. "So at the same time I'm doing a good deed, I'll also be able to see my husband."

"You're off for a few days?" I asked.

She shook her head. "We were informed that there won't be any further flights in or out by our company until this crises is over."

"Shit," Gwen said from the back. "We're going to have a hell of a time getting to the border, Keira."

"You're planning on going to the border of North Korea?" Mrs. Lee's voice was full of surprise.

"Yeah," Gwen said. "My boss in the front seat has some kind of death wish or something!"

"Gwen!" Roy's voice was a mixture of anger and surprise. "What the hell is your problem! You've been a real bitch since we landed!"

I spun around to see him staring at her with a mixture of frustration and concern.

Gwen snapped at him before I could say anything. "Problem!" She jabbed a finger at me. "She's the damn problem! We were told not to leave Canada, and here we are in Korea instead of Norway!" She pointed out the window at the darkened and deserted streets. "Look around you, Roy! The shit's going to hit the fan any minute, and here we are right in the middle of it!"

Mrs. Lee glanced into the rearview mirror at Gwen. "You may be right..." she let her voice trail off.

"What do you mean?" I said.

"Boys and toys," she sighed. "There are two armies massing at the border, their guns pointing at each other right this moment. More and more troops and equipment is arriving by the hour."

"That's not good," Roy said.

"Well... maybe they'll come to their senses?" I said hopefully.

"Nope," Roy said. "Throughout history, any time two armies face each other at a border, they always go at it."

Mrs. Lee nodded. "I heard the same thing on the television in my office before I came out to see you."

"It's like they *want* a war," I said.

"I don't know if they realized when the saber rattling started how it was going to spin out of control," said Roy. "Usually these things get to a certain point...then they take on a life of their own."

The four of us sat in silence the rest of the way to the hotel. Gwen was sitting as far away from Roy as she could in the backseat. When he reached for her hand, she slapped it away. I was beyond giving a shit about her attitude; my own thoughts were centered on the vision Sean had given me just a few days ago.

When we got to the hotel we took a suite. I dropped into my bed and stared at the ceiling.

"Nana? Oh man, Nana... if you're there, I really need your help," I said out loud to the ceiling. "Gwen's being a royal bitch, and I don't know how the hell I'm going to be able to do this with her in such a foul mood. I don't think I'll be able to do this on my own."

I waited, ears prickled, waiting for her response.

I fell asleep waiting.

Twenty Five

I DID NOT SLEEP LIKE A BABY. On the other hand, I didn't have any bad dreams, so I suppose that evened it out. I woke up groggy from jet lag, and dragged myself into the shower with my toiletry bag.

I took my time in the bathroom, even washing and blow drying my hair. I felt ungainly after being in a pressure cabin for fifteen hours, and to be completely honest I was avoiding facing the day because I didn't have the slightest idea of what to do next.

I came out of my bedroom into the living room area of the suite and stopped dead in my tracks.

Roy was curled up on the couch in the room, snoring softly. What the hell? I looked over to the room he and

Gwen had taken, but the door was closed.

Screw it. I went over and nudged him awake. "What the hell's going on?" I said in a quiet voice.

He sat up and rubbed his hands through his hair. "I dunno..." He shot a look at the bedroom where Gwen was sleeping. "We had a hell of a fight."

"What happened?" I must have fallen asleep a lot quicker than I realized because I didn't hear a thing.

"Well..." he went quiet and looked at me.

I huffed a sigh. "She told me about your secret, Roy." I felt bad for him—for both of them, actually. "Pretty crappy honeymoon, huh?"

"You're not kidding." He shook his head ruefully. "When we headed to bed... she wanted to..." his voice trailed off.

"Mess around?" I said innocently.

"Yeah. That." He looked up at me. "But I was dead on my feet and told her so." His face took on an expression of almost wonder. "She totally lost her shit! She said I was no man, and if she offered her body to me, I was *obligated*!"

"Obligated?"

"Yeah! That I *had to*..." He looked at me again. "Well, you know..."

"Perform."

He sighed. "Yeah, pretty much. I told her to drop it, that we had our entire lives to... uhhh... mess around, and that I just needed a good night's sleep." His eyes widened again. "Then she really went nuts. She said that she needed me to... you know... that she was ready and stuff." He shrugged. "I lost my own patience and told her to go take a cold shower or something." He stopped, staring off into space.

"Not the best thing to say?"

"You kidding me? She found a new level of bitch, Keira. She said stuff to me that if anyone else in the world ever said, I'd have decked them." He gestured at the couch. "I decided neutral corners was the better choice and slept out here." He looked up at me. "I mean, how could she be so terrible? Especially with what's going on in the world?"

I sat down beside him. "She's been through a lot, Roy."

He shook his head. "I don't know how I could look at her the same way again after last night."

"Oh Roy…" I put my arm around his shoulders. "Let's just get through these next few days, okay? We'll pick up the pieces after."

There was a soft knock at the door of the suite. I looked at Roy. "Did you order room service?"

"No! You woke me up, remember?"

A chill of fear shot through me like an ice pick. I crept to the door as the knocking continued. I took a quick glimpse through the peephole and gasped.

In the hallway were Shaniqua and Astrid from The Abbey! I flung the door open wide.

"OHMYGAWWD!" I cried out as I leapt into them. The three of us stood there in a group hug. The last time I had seen these women was at the bunker in Ireland where they had secreted the Indigo Children keeping them from the clutches of my now comatose grandfather, David Holmes. We had been through a real trial together, when I had been introduced to them and the Illuminata.

"Why aren't you in Norway!" I panted. "Are the kids safe? Where's Esther?"

Shaniqua laughed lightly. "Now that's what I call a welcome!" She hugged me back. "Easy, easy, Keira.

Everyone's back in Norway safe and sound. We're here because…"

"Your mother wouldn't take no for an answer," Astrid said. She ran her fingers though her hair. "From the moment she arrived, Susan made our lives miserable, telling us we were cowards hiding in Norway while you were trying to prevent this from happening. She insisted that the Illuminata find you and help you." She put her hand on my shoulder. "She's something else, Keira. Pamela's daughter through and through. She's taking good care of Esther, and…"

Shaniqua nodded. "And challenged us to be better than we were." She held out her hands. "So here we are."

I pulled them into the room to see Roy. He had met them only the one time in Ireland. As they said their hellos, I was taken aback. That entire episode only happened a couple of weeks ago. It felt like a lifetime.

"How the hell did you get here so quickly?" Roy asked. "I mean… we got here last night…"

Shaniqua smiled. "We flew all night. We've been on the go nonstop, believe me. Norway's a lot closer to Korea than Toronto, Roy."

"You must be worn out," he said.

"We slept on the plane."

"Which touched down only a half hour ago," added Astrid.

The door to Gwen's room opened, and she stepped through, fully dressed. She straightened up in surprise seeing who was there, then her head dropped lower, taking in each of us. "What's going on?"

"They're here to help," I replied.

She crossed the room, watching me, then Roy carefully.

Screw it—I reached out with my mind to probe her, but again, was rebuffed by the barrier she had been using. I didn't push it because I didn't want Gwen to sense my attempt.

She went to Roy. "I was ghastly last night, hon."

"Yeah." He pulled her to him. "Not your best night, babe." They hugged and I felt relief.

When they separated, Gwen looked at Shaniqua and Astrid. "So you're here to get us to North Korea or something? You're going to get us to their missile base?"

Shaniqua blew out a huff of air. "That's going to be a tough one, Gwen. The border's blocked off for five kilometers, and it's really, really tight security."

"Oh thank god," she replied.

"Gwen!" I said. "We have to get over the border!"

"If we can't we can't, can we?" she said. She turned back to the women. "So why don't we just head to Norway then?"

"Well…" Shaniqua looked over to me. "We have some ideas that we can work on."

Gwen crossed her arms. "Oh? Like what?"

Astrid held out a hand. "Well, the first thing we need to do is get to our sanctuary that we have here in Korea. We can discuss the details there." She turned to the windows that overlooked the city. "We don't know who's behind it, but there are elements that want this war to happen."

"And," Shaniqua continued, "we believe they consider you a threat to their objectives."

"Ya think!" I laughed. "We had a SWAT team on steroids threaten to tear my house apart just yesterday!"

"Really?"

"Yeah! They were from some military base in the U.S.A,

and came over to Canada in helicopters and four by fours!"

Shaniqua and Astrid shared a look.

Astrid took a breath and said, "Uh-oh. Brandon."

"And Brandon," Shaniqua replied. She turned to the rest of us. "Get your things; we're leaving *now*."

Twenty Six

S HANIQUA KEPT SHUSHING US while we tossed our stuff in our bags. "Say nothing right now," she said every time any of us asked a question.

When we got to the car, she murmured. "Think of your childhoods, think of your most joyful memories. You need to be in the most positive headspace you can for the next while."

"But—" I said, and she cut me off. "Those we are fighting against are drawn to pain and fear. They're looking for you; if you dwell on bad things you make it easier for them to find you." When we got in their minivan, she turned from the front seat. "Meditate on your happiest, most joyful memories from childhood. As far back as you can recall. We'll be driving for a little more than an hour."

"Where are we going?" Gwen said, her voice edgy.

"To safety. That's all I will say for now."

For the next hour or so, the four of us talked about our favorite childhood memories. We each described our favorite TV shows, family trips, good times in school, and best friends. Roy went on and on about how when he was just ten years old, his father took him up in a small plane and let him hold the wheel for a moment to give him a taste for flying.

"From that moment on, I stopped being afraid of heights and was totally hooked on becoming a pilot," he said.

I talked about how Mom and Dad never hesitated to pull me out of school and go on trips to Europe. They would get the class work from my teachers and we'd do 'school' in our hotel for an hour in the morning and again before dinner and spend the rest of the time seeing the sights and doing cool stuff.

Gwen had been silent, staring out the window, ignoring us.

I tapped her shoulder. "Your turn," I said.

Her gaze slid over to me, and she huffed a sigh. "I can't think of anything right now."

"Oh come on... who was your favorite teacher in the third grade?"

She made a strange expression. Her eyes brightened, opened wide and her eyebrows lifted; but her mouth was turned down in a frown. "Hey, you okay?" I asked. Her eyelids fluttered, and she said, "Mrs. Capra! She was the best ever! She made every day fun! I would wake up *early* on school days to make sure I didn't miss anything!"

Then her head gave a jerk, and her eyes narrowed. "I... I

can't remember any more."

I glanced up to see Shaniqua watching us in the rearview mirror. She gave a slight shake of her head. I looked at her with a question in my eyes, but she shook her head again. I looked back to Gwen to see her staring out the window again.

"Well, for me it was the fifth grade," Astrid said. "That was when I was first kissed, and it was by the nicest boy in class."

We had been traveling north, into a range of mountains. Shaniqua turned off the highway and onto a two lane road that snaked back and forth as we climbed higher into them.

"This is Bukhansan National Park," she said. I looked up at sheer stone walls that loomed over the canyon road we were in.

"The mountains are almost pure granite," she said. "Very dense, and very difficult for prying eyes and thoughts to get through." She pulled off onto a dirt path that was almost invisible from the road. "We have a sanctuary here."

We continued down the wooded path; it was so narrow that the branches of the trees scraped the side of our vehicle.

"Is this like the bunker you had in Ireland?" I asked.

"Very much so," she said.

The path ended at a small clearing. We pulled in and got out. I looked up. The trees around us made a perfect circle for the morning sky to shine through.

"This park is a mystical place," Shaniqua said. "There are ancient temples in this area. For thousands of years..." She looked at the three of us. "Long before the time of Christ, people in this region felt the pull of this area and came here to worship, meditate and wonder about the greatness of the universe. When the Illuminata began in Europe many generations ago, we heard stories of this land and came here to establish one of our first foreign Abbeys." Biting her lower lip, she continued in a soft voice. "The missionaries we sent said that this place is where our home should be, it's that mystical."

"But you didn't relocate?"

"Of course not. We began in the West, and that's our origin. But…" She raised her head and looked around. "We were welcomed here with open hearts. Being here is like looking at the stars at night."

Gwen huffed a sigh in the background. "It's the middle of the day, Shaniqua."

"You don't understand. Don't you feel it?" She saw the blank look on Gwen's face, then turned to me. "Do you, Keira? Close your eyes and feel this sacred place."

I did, and she was right. That same, well… odd emotion I would get on a summer night stargazing, rose up in me. At the same time, I felt two completely opposite experiences. I felt as insignificant as a speck of dust, and yet a sense of such grand belonging. Nodding, I opened my eyes. "Yes."

Shaniqua smiled. "We're safe within this area from those who would bring us harm."

"You mean Brandon and Brandon," I said.

She nodded. "Yes, but they act on behalf of another."

"Who?"

"We don't know. An evil force, though."

"Wait," I said, holding up my hand. "You mean like a demon?"

"Yes."

"I don't see any Abbey," Roy said, interrupting us.

Shaniqua turned to him. "No, you don't."

"Many mysteries are hidden to casual observers," Astrid added. Stepping into the circle, she made a series of gestures with her hands.

The air all around us glimmered. Bright sparks of light appeared, as if from unseen flashlights shining in our faces. The light changed colors, melding from yellow to orange and then to red. They began to lay over one another, blending into a curtain of light, bathing us in a warm, comforting glow.

"It's beautiful," I whispered. It was as wonderful as standing under a heat lamp on a snowy day. The warmth flowed over and into me, and I felt myself begin to relax and renew.

"Welcome to Humang-U-Jib" Shaniqua said. She spread her arms and the curtain parted.

A low, one-story building with a pointed roof that swept down to graceful, upturned eaves appeared before us. Thick, heavy columns held up the overhanging roof, all painted a deep red. An ornately carved marble staircase led up to the main entranceway, its doors wide open. A golden glow emitted from within.

"What does that mean?" I asked. "Humang-U-Jib?"

"House of Hope," she replied. "Come inside, but remove your shoes at the entrance."

"Why?" Gwen grumbled.

"Because you will be entering a holy place. From the dawn of time, people have removed their shoes when standing on holy ground." As she spoke, she toed her own footwear off, and the rest of us followed suit.

We entered a large airy room. Looking up, I saw the crossbeams that supported the roof were decorated with a richly colored abstract design. Golds, deep blues, reds and yellows undulated and flowed over each other in a never-ending pattern.

Thick, red cushions were arrayed in rows of circles. In the center of the room was a low table.

Shaniqua went to the table. "Here is where we will work," she said, bending and patting its surface.

Astrid pointed to a corridor at one end of the chamber. "Sleeping quarters are down there," she said. She pointed in the other direction, where another corridor went off. "Over there is the kitchen and eating facilities."

"Okay, what do we do now?" Gwen said.

"I believe that's up to Keira," Shaniqua replied.

Oh boy. I didn't have the slightest idea.

Twenty Seven

WELL, NO TIME LIKE THE PRESENT." I walked over to the low table and folding my legs under me, I lowered myself down and planted my tush on one of the cushions.

"What are you doing?" Shaniqua asked, sitting on a cushion across from me.

"I'm going to try to find the missile base."

"How?"

"I'm going to Astral Travel."

"I see." She tilted her head. "You're just going to do that."

"Umm... yeah."

Astrid came over and took a seat. "Do you need to do a cleansing ceremony?"

"No."

Shaniqua turned her head to a chest of drawers. "We have all sorts of blessed talismans that may help you."

"Help me?"

"Yes. Help you focus, get centered."

"Oh really?"

"Yes! We have herbs, teas, various incense…"

"Crystals and pyramids too, I imagine."

"Why yes!" She started to get up. "In fact, I believe there's an ancient pyramid that's made of crystal!"

I shook my head, waving her back to her seat. "Don't need it, thanks."

Gwen and Roy joined us at the table. Gwen leaned over to me. "Want me to come with you?"

"You kidding? After the last time we Astral Travelled together? No. Sean would kill me!"

Gwen made a face. "It wasn't all that bad, Keira."

My jaw dropped. "Are you kidding? You were in a coma for hours!"

She huffed a sigh. "And woke up fine, if I recall."

"Well, maybe."

She bristled. "What do you mean *maybe*?"

I wasn't actually sure what I meant, the phrase just popped out of my mouth. We stared at one another for a moment. I took a deep breath, hoping an apology or something would come out the same way.

But before I could say a word, Roy interrupted. "So how do you prepare for something like this?" he asked.

Bless his heart. I settled back down and relaxed my arms at my side. "Like this."

I closed my eyes, felt the 'pop' and was gone.

I looked down on us sitting at the table. My body was

sitting at the table, eyes closed, breathing normally. The rest of them were staring at my figure. They were all quiet as they watched me breathe.

Okey dokey.

I rose farther up until I passed through the roof of the temple. I looked down to see a clutch of pigeons roosting under one of the eaves. They sensed my passing, because one of them rose up flapping wings furiously at where my essence was, pecking at me, its beak passing through me.

Below, I saw the reason why—there were two chicks in the nest. They were older, fully feathered, not too far from having to fledge.

"Relax, Mom," I said to myself as I pulled myself higher and higher. Momma bird followed until I got too far up and turning back, swooped to her nestlings.

I eased over, and continued to rise farther and farther up, scanning the countryside to the north.

I wasn't kidding when I said I didn't have a clue.

But I had an idea.

When Gwen and I went to the hospital, and then the dentist office, I was able to sense the presence of radioactive material. I hoped that I'd be able to sense that same essence as I drifted farther and farther over the land of North Korea.

My half-baked plan was related to cooking.

I could walk into my mom's kitchen, and just sniffing the air, know if she had a roast beef in the oven, or was baking bread. Those two aromas were radically different, right? I also could tell if she was making a pot roast, or broiling steaks. Even though all three were beef, each one had its own particular scent.

I was counting on being able to sense the presence of

nuclear material, and was hoping that the deadliest of it would jump out at me the same way a loaf of fresh baked bread would light up my nose.

I headed north.

I didn't know how close I needed to be. I didn't know if I'd be able to tell the difference between a power plant and an atomic bomb. I didn't know if the lead shielding would keep me from sensing anything at all. I didn't know how far from my body I could travel safely.

I didn't have the slightest idea how much I didn't know!

But I knew one thing.

I had to *try*. I had to do the best I could with what skills, talents, gifts, or whatever the hell you call this stuff that's happened to me over the last year and a half.

Eighteen months ago I was hung over catching a subway train to my acting class. A year and a half ago I was a party girl having a wonderful time in New York City. I was rich, living on my own, and having a great time shopping, dallying with acting, and gossiping with my girlfriends. It was a simple, shallow life.

And now I was trying to save the world.

Who the hell did I think I was?

The doubt crashed over me like breaking surf.

My vision faltered, and everything began to fade. Like a computer screen dimming, the countryside below grew shadows at the edges. The landscape under me appeared grainy. Like a video out of focus, everything I was seeing was beginning to blur.

I felt myself beginning to draw back to the temple, my journey rewinding below me.

Stop! I screamed in my mind to myself. *If not me, then who?*

The scenery flowing backward below me grew still.

I was onto something.

If not now, then when? I asked myself.

Earlier in the van, heading to the sanctuary, we had been talking about school days as children. A memory of my all-time favorite teacher, from the sixth grade came to my mind. Ms. Harold was a woman in her fifties. She was by far, the kindest, strongest woman I knew until I met my Nana. We were a class of forty-five kids that year because the school had run into some kind of financial snag that led to class sizes doubling. I don't know the details—hey, I was twelve!

Forty-five 12-year-olds, six hours a day. The puberty train was pulling into the station, and this woman was the engineer, conductor, and ticket taker all rolled up into one. And I thought preventing a nuclear war was hard!

With her gray hair, stout build and clear voice she ushered us through that year with a grace and aplomb that a lion tamer would envy. It was obvious to all of us; I don't know how or why, but that woman loved each and every one of us in her class.

She had the bitchiest girl, and the toughest boy eating out of her hand with just a 'please' and 'thank you.' All of us—every single one of us—couldn't wait to get to school that day. It was the only school year of my life after kindergarten where I *welcomed* Monday mornings.

Of all the lessons learned in that class, one stood out to me starkly as I hovered over the landscape of North Korea, looking for bombs. I don't know what we were covering in class, but at one point Ms. Harold stood at the front of our room, telling us that each of us, at one point or another in our lives, would be confronted with a challenge that would scare the bejezus out of us. Extending her arm, she told us:

"When that time comes, children," she said, taking the time to make eye contact with each of us. "You're going to be scared silly. Maybe it will be when you're playing in a championship ball game. Maybe it will be when you get your first job, I don't know. But mark my words, you will have a moment in your life when the challenge before you is huge." She pointed her finger at us. "And remember this—whether you believe you can, or believe you can't, you'll be right."

"What does that mean?" someone asked. I wish it was me, but it wasn't.

"It means have faith, children. Have faith in yourselves. Especially when there's no evidence. Faith is belief when there's no evidence. Sometimes, you just gotta believe."

Sometimes, you just gotta believe.

The landscape below me snapped back into clear focus. And just as it had been on the flight over when I took Soo-jin's hand, I flew over the countryside of North Korea like a laser beam.

Twenty Eight

I COULD REMEMBER THE SICKLY GREEN COLOR OF RADIOACTIVE MATERIAL from when I was back in Kingston, so I kept my senses peeled for that aura. I rose farther up in the sky looking around me. If I was able to sense radioactive material from a CAT scanner, or a dentist's X-ray machine, the inherent evil of a nuclear warhead ought to be a snap. I rose to a height as if I was on an airliner and looked around the countryside with no success.

But then, off the coast of North Korea, in the sea, I saw the sickly glow. I couldn't understand; it was in the ocean! It was pulsating with the same bilious green pus and black tendrils, but even in daylight, it shone brightly against the surface of the sea. It was a green dome on the water, pulsing with... well, evil.

When I turned to it, I saw a second one a few miles farther out to sea. What the hell was that Kim guy doing? I aimed toward the first one, and just as I had done with Soo-jin in the search for her brother, I willed myself through the air, then into the sea.

Traveling through the murkiness of the water, I went deeper and deeper, the repulsive glow guiding me like a disgusting beacon.

It was a submarine! A long, sleek, steel tube, longer than a football field sat suspended in the depths. It wasn't moving, just sitting there motionless, like a waiting predator. The entire craft was consumed by the green aura of death.

I passed through the hull and stopped in shock.

They're Americans!

I was in a nuclear-armed submarine! The sailors and officers were all attentive to their workstations; hunched over computer screens or radar readouts as they busily prepared themselves to deliver death.

Death of a scale unimaginable...

They were all speaking English, but it was such a jumble of techno-speak jargon, they may as well have been talking in Chinese. I floated down a passageway, seeing a sign that said Missile Storage-Authorized Personnel Only! Well, I wasn't authorized, so if someone asked me to leave, I'd be okay with that... right...

I entered the missile chamber. Tube after tube lined the sides, each one practically dripping with the aura of death and despair.

When I had been on my flight over, I had read up on atomic weapons online. I learned that the bomb that blew Hiroshima to hell and back in WWII would be considered 'tiny' by today's standards. It dawned on me that the destructive power in this one submarine was enough to *incinerate* the entire island of Manhattan with just the fireballs! The blast wave and all the other destruction would destroy Long Island in just seconds, not to mention the radioactive fallout that would go on for hundreds of miles—Boston, Washington would be poisoned for hundreds of years!

And there were two of these hellish beasts parked on Korea's doorstep, not to mention what was in airplanes or crammed into huge missiles back home!

I drew back to the main control room. It was busy, but quiet as the people there busily went about their work preparing to annihilate untold millions of people.

Did they realize what they were getting ready to do?

I shot out of the submarine back up over the sea. I looked down and saw the second one, miles away. What was lying off the other coast of North Korea? What about other warships even farther out?

There were so many of them! There were so many, many bombs!

There was no freaking way I'd be able to disarm the American forces. No. Freaking. Way.

But...

I realized that I had to find Kim Whatshisname's bombs and see if I could take them out. I had read online they thought he had just a few.

Maybe if his missiles didn't work anymore, he'd back down.

I shot back over the land, searching with all my might.

As I floated over the landscape, my mind was racing. I saw just two of these submarines, but I knew that the States had more. And so did Russia! And how many countries had these bombs? I knew that China did, but didn't England too? And France? What about India? They had some, and so did Pakistan right next door; and those two countries hated each other!

I was astonished that human beings had survived as long as we had.

I came to a stop, suspended above the countryside. What the hell was I doing here in the first place? Why the hell should I be here? What's wrong with us that a situation like this is even considered?

And who the hell did I think I was to think I could do *anything* about this?

The images Sean had flashed in my mind. A blinding, white blast, followed by a rolling maw of black, oily flame crashing through trees, buildings, homes... and screaming people shot through my mind.

Leaving only death and darkness in its wake. Black, utter darkness...

I grasped for anything hopeful to cling to as scene after scene of pain... no, agony, of suffering of all kinds rolled through my mind. Those who survived, by some miracle, trying to care for the injured as the fallout poisoned them all... as a dark night descended.

Go on, Keira... it's better to light a single candle than waste time cursing the darkness! You must, MUST go on!

I jerked at the sound of Nana's voice in my mind. "Nana?" I reached out to her presence, but felt nothing.

But really... that was all I needed. Whether she had reached out to me, or it was my imagination, it didn't matter. I knew what I had to do next.

I centered myself, and reached out through the landscape

below me with an aching longing to find Kim's own cache of evil. From my experience with the submarine I had a better idea of what I was seeking. Through mountains and valleys, across forests and fields, I sought that same disgusting pestilence, searching the countryside far and wide.

A row of three circles on the ground appeared to me. They were nestled in a deep canyon, with a narrow opening to the sky above, but there was no mistaking them. They were not as bright as the submarine, but they were the same color. Looking down, I saw that there was a row of three circles, in a straight line, hundreds of yards apart from each other.

I was looking down at the caps of missile silos.

I descended down toward the closest one. Gotta start somewhere, right? As effortlessly as I had entered the submarine, I was within the silo. I didn't bother taking a tour like I had on the sub, I went straight to the nose cone of the missile, the source of the glow.

Passing through the outer skin, my spirit was within the warhead. It was no effort to determine what all the parts and components were; the disgusting glow brightened as I drew closer to it. I found two spheres, one nestled within the other, ringed with a perfect symmetry of explosives. At the right moment, the explosives would detonate, forcing the outer sphere to slam into the inner one. The two pieces of radioactive material would instantaneously reach a critical mass and detonate into a nuclear explosion.

But only if they struck one another with absolutely perfect timing. If there was the smallest crack or wrinkle; any imperfection in their shapes, just like a soufflé failing to rise in an oven, they would simply break apart instead.

So all I had to do was will the metals into disruption. A

simple case of mind over matter.

I got this.

Hell, if I could talk ghosts into crossing The Veil, move glasses of water by just thinking about it, this should be a piece of cake, right? I focused on the gleaming metal.

Nothing.

Not just no results, but I had the feeling I was doing no more than sighing into a windstorm. When I did telekinesis in the past, I could *feel* the glass as I tried to move it. When I zorched those computers back in Kingston, I felt the... essence of the devices with my mind as soon as I focused on them. This time though, there wasn't any sort of feedback loop between me and the warhead. I focused on it, and felt no connection at all.

It was such a disgusting, hateful device! All it was meant to do was destroy! Its reason for coming into existence, the reason people invented it, and then built this thing was to create horror and death! I bore down on it with all my will; hating it for its nature.

I tried with all my might, but nothing changed. The aura around that thing remained steady in its glow; if anything it pulsed even brighter as I poured my energy into a force of will to destroy it.

Without warning, everything began to fade to black. It started at the edges, and in just a moment I couldn't see anything at all! I snapped back to my body.

At the instant I returned, a wave of utter exhaustion overtook me. I sat up, struggling to keep my eyes opened, but fell over into a well of darkness.

Twenty Nine

WHEN I OPENED MY EYES, a plush duvet covered me. Oh man, my head was pounding like I had thrown back a dozen gin gimlets. Slowly, I brought my hands to my face to grind the sleep from them. My lips felt like two strips of leather. Oh man... I eased up from the bed, every muscle in my body aching. Good grief, I'd been put through the wringer.

Although the window to my bedroom was covered with a heavy curtain, I could see bright morning sunlight bleeding through the edges. How long was I asleep? Asleep? Passed out was a better description. I staggered out, walking gingerly to the bathroom.

My hands grazed a long nightshirt. Someone had undressed me and put me to bed. Dying of thirst, I wandered down the corridor back to the main room.

Shaniqua saw me first, leaping up and running to my side, a look of deep worry on her face.

"How are you feeling?" she asked.

"Like I was hit by a truck," I mumbled. She took my arm and guided me to the kitchen area and helped me sit in a normal chair. Thank goodness—there was no way I'd be able to lower myself onto those cushions on the floor in the main room.

Shaniqua nodded to Astrid, who had followed us in. "Let Gwen know she's up." As Astrid left, she turned back to me. "Can I get you something?"

"I'm terribly thirsty," I said.

She nodded. "I have just the thing."

"Oh lord, please no mumbo-jumbo, higher-plane organic joy juice…"

She smiled. "How about ordinary OJ?"

"Perfect." She poured me a full glass, and I drained it in a single pull.

Astrid returned, and Gwen was right behind her.

Gwen stood at the entranceway, her arms folded. "What the hell did you do to yourself? You look like shit."

Roy came up behind her. "Take it easy, hon. She's been asleep for fourteen hours."

Gwen's mouth pursed. "Did you take some drugs or something?"

"No! What the hell?" She was looking at me like this was all my fault! I could see how she was Asshat Sean's sister right then, let me tell you. No, 'I was worried.' No, 'are you okay?' Just coming down on me for trying to do the right thing. I shook my head. Slowly. It was aching like mad.

"You guys have any aspirin in this place?" I asked Astrid.

"I'll check the first-aid kit; I'm sure we do." She left for the bathroom.

"You're dehydrated," Shaniqua said as she poured me

another OJ. "I guess it's to be expected after that long flight, but you were in pretty good shape until you Astral Travelled."

"It's not jet lag," I said.

"Did you find them?" Roy asked. When I nodded, he said, "Where are they? How many of them are there? Were you able to wreck 'em?"

I took another sip of the OJ. It was ambrosia. I could feel the sweet, cold liquid revitalize me as it went down into my stomach. Putting the glass down I shook my head slowly.

"I found lots of atom bombs," I said.

"What? How many does he have?" Gwen said.

"Kim's got three, but I also came across two American submarines hiding out in the Yellow Sea to the east of here. Each one of them has more than a dozen nuclear bombs. Big ones"

"What the hell were you doing spying on the Americans?" Gwen asked sharply. "Your job was to find the North Korean nukes!"

"What the hell is the matter with you Gwen?" I snapped back. "You've become a royal bitch, you know that?"

The room went still as we stared at each other. Gwen huffed a sigh. "I didn't come halfway around the world to get blown to smithereens!" she said. She spun on her heels and stormed out of the kitchen.

Roy's eyes followed her out, but he stayed in the room. He turned back to me. "She's just scared, Keira."

"And I'm wrung out," I said.

I told them all that had happened; the two submarines off the coast loaded for bear, and the three missiles I found in a canyon. And about my miserable failure to accomplish anything.

When I finished, Roy said, "Okay, what's next?"

"I don't know, Roy," I replied, shaking my head slowly. "I'm out of ideas, and I'm beat to a snot from trying."

"Well, the first thing is to get some food into you," Astrid said. "You haven't eaten since yesterday—"

"Two days, actually," I said. "I had something light on the flight over, and that's the last time I ate."

She got up and started rummaging in the fridge. "Okay then. Eggs it is."

"What time is it?" I asked.

"Seven a.m.," Shaniqua said. "You passed out yesterday afternoon at around three p. m."

"But it was morning when we got here!" I didn't think I had spent *that* much time on the Astral Plane.

"You were entranced for hours, Keira," Roy said. "I wanted to wake you, but they didn't think that would have been a good idea."

"Then you came to and keeled over," Shaniqua said. "We put you to bed and checked on you every hour. You didn't move one bit after we put you in bed."

"Yeah… I don't understand that. I tried with everything I had to damage those warheads, but didn't affect them at all. Then everything began to fade on me while I was there, and I came back here. It felt like I wasn't even gone an hour."

"Time's different in that plane, Keira," Shaniqua said.

"Well, I'll have something to eat and try again." I glanced up to see Gwen had returned. "I'm going to need your help, Gwen."

She looked at me with steely eyes. "Not a chance in hell."

Thirty

MY JAW DROPPED. "WHAAAT?"

"I'm out of here," she said. "I'm going back to the airport, find a flight, or else charter a plane on the credit card you set up for me. I'm heading for Norway. This is way too far out of hand for me to stick around. And if you couldn't accomplish anything, what makes you think I could?"

"We'll go together, of course!" I leaned forward. "You know my powers always, *always* increase when you and I are together!" I held out my hand. "You take my hand, and I'm stronger, better, and everything I do is increased! You know this!"

She shook her head. "Not this time. You think you can save the world, be my guest." She turned to Roy. "Come on,

Roy."

"Gwen..."

"I SAID, COME ON!" she roared at him.

Roy stood his ground and turned beet red. I watched as he clenched and unclenched his fists. "I don't know what your problem is Gwen," he said in an even voice. "You're acting like a fool. We're trying to do some pretty damn important work here, and you've been a bitch on wheels since we left Canada! What the hell is wrong with you?"

"You're my husband!" she spat out.

"Not for long! As soon as I get back to Canada I'm getting this marriage annulled!"

It was like water off the back of a duck. "Fine," she said. I was amazed at how well she took it. They just got married, and now they're splitting up?

"Wait a minute guys," I said. "Roy, why don't you drive her to the airport, okay? And if you decide to leave too, I won't hold it against you." I nodded toward Gwen. "She *is* your wife after all; you *did* make a vow."

He shook his head. "I don't know who the hell she is, Keira." He stepped up to Gwen. "If this is who you really are, you sold me a lie. You're not the girl I met a year ago." He gave a short wave. "Bon voyage, Gwen."

I watched Gwen's face for any sign of sadness or regret, but there wasn't any. Her lips were a thin line, and her eyes steely as she looked from Roy to each of us standing there, ending with me.

"I'll give your regards to your parents," she said.

A chill went through me.

"And... *Esther* too, of course."

"Hey... Gwen..." I said.

But she turned on her heels and left. I looked over at

Roy. He watched her leave with a stony face. When we heard the van start up, his face collapsed and he crumpled onto one of the kitchen chairs, holding his head in his hands.

"What did I just dooo…" he moaned.

Astrid and Shaniqua had watched the entire exchange without saying a word, and they stood there, not knowing what to do. I flew beside him and put my arms around him. "She's scared, Roy. People do crazy things when they panic."

He took a deep breath and lifted his head. "You didn't." He gestured at the two women. "They're not running away. She's chickening out. And…" He shook his head slowly. "I can't respect a coward."

"I'm scared too, Roy," I said quietly. I was already missing the closeness of what Gwen and I shared in friendship over this last year. I was desperately trying to hang on to the Gwen whom I grew to love, and didn't want Roy to toss that away either.

"You're scared? Ha! I'm terrified!" he replied. "But you know what, Keira? We're *brave*. We're not letting our fear tell us what we can or can't do. We know we're doing the right thing. Shit, we're the only ones who have a chance at defusing this nightmare!" He looked around the room. "And if we fail, we're probably going to die here; you know that, right?"

I nodded. Especially after seeing those submarines. Fingers were on triggers and were really itchy. If I couldn't figure out a way to render Kim's missiles harmless, somebody on one side or another will step over some kind of line and… boom. We wouldn't have time to get away. "I think you're right, Roy."

He looked over at Shaniqua and Astrid. "You guys think the same, right?" When they nodded back, Astrid's eyes were wide in fear and brimming with tears. He nodded sharply to them and turned back to me. "So we know the stakes. And we're sticking."

Astrid spoke softly. "To run and hide now... that would be a greater crime."

"Yup. That would be *cowardly*," he said. He turned back to me. "I'm not as gifted as you, Keira. I can't do any of that..." He fluttered his hands in the air. "That wooo-wooo ghosty shit you and Gwen can do." He leaned toward me. "But I'm just as damned brave as you."

I stood and cradled his head against me. "Maybe you're braver, Roy." Gwen, you're such a fool. Astrid and Shaniqua crossed the room and encircled the two of us with their arms in what must have been a ridiculous-looking group hug.

But it gave me strength. I felt their energy—their hope, love, and ultimately faith in what we were trying to do, and it filled me with renewed warmth.

Which gave me an idea.

Thirty One

O KAY," I SAID, "LET'S GET TO WORK." I
disentangled myself from their hug and stepped
away. "We need to get back to it."

"But... you're exhausted, Keira," Shaniqua said.

I gave my head a small shake. "Not anymore. Let's go." I
turned and headed back to the main room. Nothing had
changed; three circles of cushions around a heavy table were
in the center. The table was quite large, you could easily fit
ten or more people around it, and that was too big for my
needs. I pulled a series of cushions at the outside circle,
making a small square.

They had followed me, but were standing at the
passageway as I pulled and placed the enormous cushions in
place. They were like overstuffed beanbags; comfortable as

hell when you sat in them, but ungainly as anything to move around.

"Keira…" Shaniqua said, "what are you doing?"

"Rearranging the furniture, of course!" I joked. When I was satisfied with the placement, I plopped down onto one of the spots. I gestured to them to take their places.

"What's the plan, boss?" Roy said as he sat beside me.

"I'm going back in, but all of you are coming with me."

"Whoa, whoa, whoa!" he said, stiffening. I don't know nuthin' about Astral Travellin' Miz Swanson!" Nevertheless, he stayed in place.

"I know," I said. "But… I pointed with my chin at Shaniqua and Astrid. "They're familiar with it—"

"I've done a little, yes," Shaniqua said, "but Astrid…" she looked over at her.

"I've never been able to get as far as separation into the plane, Keira," Astrid said. "I tried and tried, but that's not a skill I was ever able to develop."

Both of them stood still, looking at me dubiously.

I shrugged. "It doesn't matter. I don't know if you'll be able to Astral Travel or not, okay? But one thing I realized back in the kitchen was that we give each other energy." I cast my gaze over each of them. "You all felt it when we hugged, back there, didn't you?"

"Yeah…" Roy said. "It was pretty cool…" He looked off into space. "It was like being with Gwen, but without getting horny." His hand flew to his mouth. "Shit. Sorry. I didn't mean that to come out that way!"

"It was agapé, Roy," Astrid said as she took a place beside him.

"Aga-pay?"

"Yes, it's a form of love… the highest form. That's what

we all shared in there." She looked over at me. "I felt it too."

I didn't know there was a name for it, but I nodded. Shaniqua and Astrid had spent their lives exploring the depths and wonders of the human condition beyond what we normally see, hear, taste and smell... and touch. And as far as I knew, our vaunted science and technological culture didn't spend a lot of effort on this life-affirming, life-giving aspect of being human.

"Greater love does not exist," Shaniqua said. "It's powerful..." She sat beside Astrid.

Well, if there was one thing I needed, it was power. I had tried with all my might to disable that warhead and didn't put a dent in it. I held out my hands; one to Roy and the other to Astrid. "I need the power of your love, guys. I'm going to Astral Travel again, but I want us all joined when I do."

Roy clasped my hand in his. "Any idea what's gonna happen to us when you... *launch*?"

"No."

"This could be dangerous then."

"I really don't know, Roy. Maybe." When I Astral Travelled with Gwen, she went into that coma, right?" It had happened when we were in the middle of battling my grandfather David Holmes, now in a vegetable state. Gwen and I were searching for the Indigos, and Astral Travelled to see if we could find them. We entered the plane together, but somehow our souls... our spirits?... became separated. I thought I lost her, but she did come back. I took a breath. "Probably."

He nodded thoughtfully. "Yeah, that's what I suspected." He gave my hand an extra squeeze. "Ready when you are, Keira." He closed his eyes, his breath quickening with tension.

Taking Astrid's hand, Shaniqua said, "Well, it's probably going to be a hell of a ride for you, Roy." She made a quick smile, and both of them closed their eyes.

I centered myself and closed my own eyes. *Oh boy, Nana... anything you can do?* I sent that prayer out, but there was no reply. Rats. Okay.

I took several deep breaths, letting each out slowly. Okay then, here we go.

Pop.

Thirty Two

TOGETHER, STILL HOLDING HANDS, the four of us rose through the ceiling and above into the bright sunshine of the morning. Roy and the others were a translucent gold; I could see through them as if they were a rain-streaked window, to the area below.

Roy, let go of Shaniqua's hand, let's form a row instead of a circle. His eyes widened as he received my thought and opened his opposite hand. His other hand felt firm in my own. Which was a little weird. I was out of my body, but was still able to feel his hand in mine, and Astrid's, with my other hand.

We rose higher and higher, seeing the earth begin to curve below us and to the horizon.

Look over that way, I said, jerking my head toward the sea. From even that great distance of miles and miles, the sickly green glowing aura of the closest missile submarine stood out like a beacon of impending doom. *Their aura is even stronger, they must be on alert.*

Or countdown, Keira! Roy's thought sent a chill through me. *Let's get this show on the road!*

He was right! I turned toward the north, and with all my will, pushed us forward. I knew where I was heading now, and wasn't going to waste a second.

The land below us went past in a blur, and we were above the canyon where the silos were. Oh no...

When I was there the last time, their glow had been muted. Now, each of the silos emitted the same harsh green aura, with pulsating ripples of purplish black.

Shaniqua's presence voiced in my head. *Something must have happened, Keira. The North Koreans are incredibly angry!* The same purple and black tendrils soaking through the glow of the missile silos were snaking through the buildings of the base. *Those people below are enraged. That's what's causing the aura color below.*

It's worse than that guys, came from Roy. *They have the silo hatches open. They're warming up to fire those things!*

I looked down to the silos to see he was right. When I had seen the glow from the silos, I hadn't noticed the change. Now, looking below, I could see tendrils of vapor wafting up from the opened hatches.

Kim's fueling the missiles, Roy's thoughts sent a chill through me. *These guys are getting ready.*

I shot down into the first silo, yanking them with me with my sudden move. We entered, and were at the top of the nose cone. It was pulsing and oozing its aura of horror.

Oh! Astrid cried out. *The death and pain in this... this THING!*

It's a disgusting and hateful thing, I replied. *Let's break it!* Leaning forward, I focused my hatred and disgust with this beastly machine. *Concentrate!* I commanded. We all bent forward, sending our anger and frustration out to it.

And not a damn thing happened. I could see the inner workings, the perfect spheres, and with the will of the four of us, I expected it to crack, or at least quiver under our combined onslaught.

But nothing was happening!

I felt both Roy's and Astrid's hands tremble in mine with their effort. I was shaking, I was trying so hard. *Why isn't this working!* my mind cried out. I kept at it, but began to feel myself again grow weary.

Be still, Keira, Shaniqua's voice echoed within me. *Everyone, stop trying to destroy it.*

But we gotta! Roy cried out.

We came this far, Shaniqua! called Astrid. *Only to fail?*

Fear and horror overcame us, and I was probably leading the parade.

Shaniqua released Roy's hand and floated over to me. Suspended before me, she looked into my eyes. Her deep-brown eyes gazed into mine as she drew her hand up and stroked the side of my face. *I have an idea...* she said. *Please, be at peace, and have faith in the Universe.*

The touch of her hand in this realm was even more comforting than it had been back at The Sanctuary. I closed my eyes and reveled in it. A sense of gentleness, but also surprising strength filled me. I opened my eyes, understanding now.

Agapé, I said.

Yes... She turned to the others and performed the same gestures. As she did, Shaniqua spoke in our minds and hearts. *We do not possess enough hatred in our souls to match the evil before us. It is but a machine, and yet its inherent nature is one of destruction, unimaginable terror, and uncountable death. We cannot battle with such a creation with anger or hatred; its own evil is far stronger than what we could conceive.*

So what the hell are we supposed to do? Roy asked.

We do not contend with it, like-for-like. We overwhelm it with what it lacks so utterly. Shaniqua began to glow bright. *Love, in all its splendor and joy is a far, far greater power than this horrible, pathetic beast.* She turned to the warhead. *Show it how powerless it is before the greatest power of the Universe. Bathe it in love...*

In Agapé, added Roy.

Shaniqua floated from him and took his hand. *Let us begin...*

Oh you horrible, poor thing, I thought. *Your nature is so one-sided. You are not a farmer's plow, or even a carpenter's saw. You cannot build, or create, only destroy. A sewing needle, a simple pin and thread creates more in its time here than you ever will, despite your massive power. You poor, horrible thing.*

I thought of my parents; if I never saw them again, they would still love me for all eternity. I thought of Esther, and the life I wanted to build for her. I thought of Gwen, and how my love for her was the cause of the pain I felt when she left us.

I thought of my Nana.

And felt so utterly blessed. So utterly, profoundly blessed. Tears of gratitude and joy filled my eyes as I stared at that warhead. That poor thing, never in its existence would it ever be able to create or support life.

There was no poof, bang, or anything. It pulsed for an instant, cracks appearing along its surface. As if it was being draped in a layer of gauze, the cracks and imperfections multiplied and spread until the entire surface of that once perfect, gleaming sphere looked like it was a child's sand sculpture on a beach.

And just like that, it crumbled to dust.

The control wires that had been attached fell away, and in that instant alarms blared.

One down, two to go.

Still holding one another's hands, we transferred to the second missile. Having an idea of how to do this, we turned it to dust in no time flat. The cacophony of alarms and sirens blared even louder, and I heard a voice thunder in Korean over the loudspeaker. I didn't speak the language, but I didn't need a translator to hear the panic and rage in the voice as it barked out orders.

Good luck with that, buster! I smiled inwardly. This was going to work!

Just as I was about to urge us to the final missile, Astrid's essence let out a pealing scream in my mind. I looked to her to see her face contort in anguish before she vanished in a blink.

Uh-oh.

Thirty Three

"WHAT THE HELL JUST HAPPENED?" I asked Shaniqua.

Her own eyes were wide in shock and dismay. *We're under attack at the Sanctuary!* was all she could get out before blinking away too.

I looked over at Roy. Confusion and fear covered his face before he too blinked away.

I floated alone in the silo. What the hell was going on? I needed to get back to the Sanctuary! I thrust myself away from the silo, and in no time at all snapped back into my body and opened my eyes.

To a blazing inferno.

The Sanctuary was filled with flame and smoke. Astrid, Shaniqua, and Roy lay on their cushions unconscious. What the hell had just happened? I staggered to my feet, and immediately bent over retching. The fumes almost overwhelmed me, but I dropped to the floor where I was sure it would be less poisonous.

I scrabbled over to Roy's form. His eyes had rolled up inside his head, only the whites showing, and he was barely breathing. What the hell had happened?

I pushed and shoved at him, calling his name. "Roy! Wake up! We have to get out of here!" But he wasn't moving. I scrabbled over to Shaniqua and Astrid only to find they too were both out cold. Oh shit.

At the noise of cracks that sounded like pistol shots, my head jerked up. The solid beams of the roof were engulfed in billowy flames, and were beginning to bow downward as the hungry fire fed on them. Ashes and hot cinders rained down on us.

I grabbed Astrid's wrist and sucked a deep breath by the floor. I stood up and staying as hunched over as possible, dragged her from the sitting area and out the front of the building. I pulled her away from the building about twenty feet and ran in for Roy. When I got to the doorway, the heat drove me to my knees.

Looking into the room, I saw the overhead beams crack and drop toward the floor where Roy and Shaniqua were lying.

"NO!" I screamed with my entire being.

A knife of pain shot through my head. It was the most excruciating sensation I had ever felt. A thick rod of silvery agony pierced from the back of my skull, out over my eyebrows. A red veil colored my vision. The intensity of it made me stop breathing.

It also froze the burning timbers in midair.

On my hands and knees I crawled to them. I sat on the floor between them and reached out, grasping a wrist in each hand. Like I was on a rowing machine, I pushed with my feet against the floor, inching my way back toward the door. They were so heavy.

I kept my eye on the suspended flaming heap in the air above us, as over and over I pushed with my feet, inching us out toward the door.

I could feel my lungs burning from the heat and ashes floating in the air. My skin was turning red, like a sunburn in fast motion. I dropped my head and grunted with each shove of my feet against the floor.

"Not today!" I growled out loud at death. "Not todaaay!"

If I made it out of here I was going to be telling Roy he had to lose some weight.

My legs quivered with effort as I pulled us over the threshold of the door. A cinder from the transom dropped onto the back of my neck; I could feel the skin at the spot where my spine met my neck begin to sizzle. Oh shit that hurt!

I yelped, and with a final shove of adrenaline and agony, lunged through the door, dragging Roy and Shaniqua with me like a pair of oversized Raggedy Ann dolls. We rolled off the portico just as my strength left me. The spike of agony in my head disappeared at the same instant the timbers crashed to the floor in an explosion of flaming wood.

Flames licked out the entranceway at us. I got on my knees and rolled Roy farther away from the entrance, scrabbled back and did the same with Shaniqua. As I rolled her away, I saw her clothes were smoking. I looked down at my blouse to see that it was also just on this side of bursting into flames too.

I gaped at the flaming ancient structure. It was fully consumed, smoke reaching up to the sky, with embers like fireflies in the daytime, swept into the updraft. What the hell had happened?

"Who the hell *did* this?" I said out loud.

"Oh. That was us, Keira!" Brandon and Brandon said in unison from behind me.

Oh boy.

Thirty Four

MY NECK CREAKED AS MY HEAD PIVOTED to look over my shoulder. When I saw them, I let out a sigh. Same sunglasses, same black suits and ties with white shirts… *Do they have any idea what kind of clichés they are?* I asked myself. 'Men In Black? Puh-leeze…

They stood leaning against one of those huge Suburbans, also as black and shiny as their suits.

I shook my head slowly. "You look like you're auditioning for the next *Mission Impossible* movie, you know."

Brandon flashed a smile of huge white, perfect teeth. "We do what we can," he said, pushing himself away from the vehicle's side. Keeping his face toward me, he reached behind himself and opened the back passenger door. "Found something," he said. "Want to see?"

The door opened wide, and sitting there, eyes wide, was Gwen.

I staggered to my feet. "What have you done to her?

Why are you doing this?"

The other Brandon made a show of looking at his watch. "Just giving ol' Kim up north the chance to get his act together and get this show on the road." He nodded to his partner. "I think it'll just be a little while, and he'll get that last one off the ground."

The other Brandon nodded. "And our work will be done." He rubbed his hands briskly. "And then the real fun will begin!"

"You want this to happen! You want a nuclear war to start!" I was on my feet, but barely. My knees were knocking and the memory of the agony in my head from my telekinesis during the fire left me weak as a kitten.

The Brandon holding the door to the vehicle open jerked his head. "Of course, silly!"

"But… but *why*?" I looked at Gwen. She was still as a statue, watching me. What had they done to her?

"Sweet and sour of course!" the same Brandon replied.

I gaped at him. "Whaaat?"

He held out his hand, palm up. "Sweet." He flipped his hand over. "Sour." He flipped it back. "Light," he said. Turning it back over, he said, "Dark." He flipped it palm up again. "Life." And flipping it over, said "Death."

The other Brandon chimed in. "We're the 'other side,' Keira. People and beings like you work for life, and goodness, and all sorts of nicey-nice things…" He tilted his head toward his partner. "We on the other hand recognize that without darkness, there can be no light. Without death, what is life after all?" He shrugged. "We're just part of the balance needed, that's all!"

Brandon by the door nodded. "And we soooo love our work!"

The world spun around me. "Millions will die..." I whispered, my voice as raspy as The Sanctuary's walls groaned just before collapsing onto themselves.

Brandon by the car door shrugged. "So? Big deal, Keira. You know that..." He waved his hands. "All this is just one stage. You, better than anyone knows that these..." his voice took a bitter edge, "these primates, these... *monkeys* have souls and will go on, so what's the big deal?" He shook his head. "Nope, we're just hurrying them along a path already set for them."

"Nobody wants to die, asshole! What if someone tried to kill you and move *you* along?"

"Did you hear what she just said, Brandon?" They shot one another a look and burst out laughing.

While they were distracted, I sent a thought to Gwen. *Get out of there and help me! We can take these two on!* She stared at me and shook her head no. What in the world was happening?

"Look, Keira," one of the Brandons said. "We..." He gestured at himself and his partner. "We can't die, okay? We're not of this plane. We're here at our master's behest to... well, like I said, 'speed things along.' Your species... well, there's a whole school of thought that believes you... *humans* have gotten wayyy too big for your britches and need to be taken down a peg or two. We're here to get you out of your..." He gestured at the air.

"Out of your high-rise condos," the other Brandon said.

"Yeah! And out of your sports cars!"

"And your airplanes!"

"And... and turn off your TVs!"

"And iPhones!"

They were nodding to one another in agreement as they

kept up their litany of modern life, and finally finished, turning back to me and saying in unison, "And get back into the trees where you belong like the monkeys you are!"

Gwen leaned out of the car. "How much longer?" she called to them.

The Brandon beside her adjusted his sunglasses and looked off into space. "Just a few minutes. Kim's getting the missile ready to go; he's retargeting it to Hawaii." He snorted. "He's aiming for Pearl Harbor!"

"As soon as they confirm the trajectory..." The other Brandon snickered, looking at me. "All those submarines will launch their full complement of missiles at North Korea..."

"And the ball will start rolling!" The Brandon beside Gwen did a little jig.

"Start? What do you mean start?"

"Duh! Silly girl! Who lives right next door to North Korea, huh?"

"China?" Oh no. I went cold.

"Bingo! Give that girl a prize! They're going to see all these nukes heading from the submarines, right next door to them, and... well... they won't be too happy."

"China will sinka' da subs!" his partner said.

"And den de 'Merican's will fire on China!"

They both started capering; hooking their arms with each other and spinning in a circle doing a jig like a pair of drunken cowboys. "Before ya know it, Russia will be a launchin'! Then France! Then the U.K.! Everyone with a nuke is either gonna let theirs fly, or else they're gonna be left out!"

They stopped and faced me. "It'll be known as 'The Big Ka-Boom'! Wipe the slate clean an' start all over again!" one of them said. I don't know which one was which. And it doesn't really matter. They were drunk on their imminent spectacle.

"You'll die too…"

"No… as soon as the first one goes off over Korea, we'll just transition back to our plane of existence, silly." He snorted. "We'll have a ringside seat for all the fun! But…" He pointed at me. "You? Hmmm… not so much." He flashed that grin at me again.

I needed to get into the Astral Plane and get back to the missile site!

I lowered myself to the ground. The two Brandons watched me.

"Grab her!" Gwen said. "She can't Astral Travel if you hold on to her!"

"Yes ma'am!" they said as they leapt at me. *Gwen?* My mouth dropped open as Brandon and Brandon grabbed me by the arms and yanked me to my feet.

I stood there shaking as Gwen alighted from the backseat.

It wasn't Gwen.

Reading my thoughts, she shook her head sadly. "Oh dear, no. I took over this body from Gwen when I left your grandfather David, Keira. I got my first whiff when I trapped her in the Astral Plane. Just enough to create a space for me to flee to should things with your grandfather go badly." She made a face. "And they did. I didn't expect that sniveling child who gave him that aneurysm to be so damn powerful!"

I recoiled at the memory. David Holmes, my grandfather, had been my nemeses. He had kidnapped Gwen and Roy in an effort to get me to join him in his megalomaniacal delusion to rule the world. He had left a path of destruction and death in his wake—even the death of a daughter he never knew he had.

But it wasn't just him. This… *thing*, this demon from somewhere out there had entered him and taken him over. David *had* been born with paranormal gifts, and according to Nana, had an ego just as big as his gifts. His thirst for power had been the crack in his soul where this beast had entered him.

But *Gwen*? How did this beast gain control over her?

The thing with Gwen's face smiled at me. "You made it possible, dear. Her so-called 'brother' warned you about Astral Travel, but you went ahead anyway, taking her along for the ride! She was easy pickings… I created a small nest for me in the Astral Plane… aaaand moved in when I needed to! She put up a bit of a fight, but she's tucked into a corner."

"No!" I barked. "Gwen, if you're in there, fight this beast!" I felt so stupid as I said the words. As if she wouldn't have done everything she could to ward off this demon.

"Brandon?" Gwen said. "How are things progressing in the north?" She kept her eyes on me.

He tilted his head, staring off into space. "Pretty good, actually. They've gotten all the systems back online and are going through the final checklists." He rubbed his hands together. "This is going to make Hiroshima look like a party balloon popping!"

Gwen stared at me. "Yes," she said, smiling. "It most certainly will." I noticed a glowing brightness behind her eyes. The energy and power that infected Gwen was immense.

"Gwen... please..." I said. "Life is all we know..."

"I'm not Gwen. Would you like to know my name?"

One of the Brandons stiffened. "Uh oh... I don't think that's a good idea, boss. You can't give her your name, remember? That's your weak spot!"

She brushed a hand at him. "Pish and tush, Brandon. It's been eons since I said my name out loud on this plane." She turned back to me and eyed me with mirth. "Listen well..."

Bending her neck, she opened her mouth to the sky.

The sound that emanated from her was deafening. Every wail of sorrow, fear and regret in all of human history welled from her in a shrieking high-pitched bellow. It enveloped my body, echoed off the surrounding mountains like an explosion of misery.

The air went still in its aftermath, like the entire world was in shock saying, 'what the hell was *that*?'

"Whoaaaa, boss," the other Brandon said. "Haven't heard that one in quite... some... time!"

Gwen... or whatever it was, dropped her chin and batted her eyes at him. "Why thank you, Brandon!"

She turned to me with a sardonic smile.

But before she could speak, the entire area was suddenly awash in a golden, beautiful light. All around us the surrounding area emitted a warm glow. The plants, my own hands, even the burning embers of The Sanctuary were all painted over with hues of yellows, golds and bright-white lights.

Gwen's eyes flashed wide.

"Uh-oh," said Brandon.

Thirty Five

WELL, GARAMOD, YOU HAD TO GO AND
SHOW OFF!" SEAN stood there in a golden
aura. "Whatever made you think we wouldn't
hear that?" he shook his head in bewildered pleasure. "I
didn't have a clue you had taken over my sister until just
now!"

"Ohhh... shit!" Brandon and Brandon said in unison.
"God damn it!" They turned to Gwen. "You hadda open
your biiiig mouth!"

I had fallen and now propped myself up on my elbows,
watching. My mouth was opening and closing slowly as I
took in what was going on.

Standing in the middle of the golden hue, were Sean and
Cora Gaines.

Cora Gaines?

Swirling around them were golden, white and glittery speckles. Like fireflies in the daytime, they made ribbons of beauty and swirled like translucent ribbons all around us. I held out my hand, and one of the ribbons flowed around it. Looking over my shoulder, I saw them flow over and through the still unconscious forms of Roy, Astrid and Shaniqua, caressing them gently.

I turned my head back to the group before me.

Gwen's mouth was turned down in a frown, and her eyes were hard. Her hand rose pointing at Sean and Cora.

Oh. Yeah. Sean and Cora looked kinda different...

You know...

Actually you don't. Let me see...

They were wearing white gowns with golden threads woven through the fabric so they gleamed and sparkled in the light. Actually, they were emitting light. You know that warm, golden light I mentioned? Yeah... it was emanating from the two of them. They were two brilliantly beautiful lanterns, suffusing all around them in a warm, comforting radiance.

Looking at Gwen, Sean's face had an expression I could only describe as loving exasperation. Cora's face was a gentle smile as she too looked at the beast that was not Gwen.

Her once steel-gray hair that had been tied up in a severe bun was now flowing over her shoulders in auburn waves. Where her face had been lined with the *well* over forty-plus years of age, there was now smooth, shining, *perfect* skin. She didn't look a day over twenty to boot. *Twenty?*

The bitch was stunningly beautiful; sorry, but I was jealous. The Cora I knew was just some kind of disguise. I wanted to hate her, but...

I couldn't. Not really. The glow from her was a pulsing presence of goodness. Kindness and... *love*, dammit, flowed from her like a visible mist. As she took Gwen/Garamod in with her eyes, her smile was gently loving, but had an element of firmness; like a frustrated parent of a smart-aleck kid. She closed and opened her eyes slowly while giving her head a shake.

Turning from Gwen, she looked over at me. Her head dipped in acknowledgment of my presence.

"You did well, Keira," she said, and looked to Sean. "Don't you agree?"

"Of course," he said. "We're almost done here." He looked over at the Brandons and let out a sigh. "Okay, fellas, off with you, now."

"NO!" shouted Gwen, her voice having that same terrible roar and thunder from before.

Cora raised her hand like a traffic cop. "That's enough, Garamod." She put her finger to her lips. "Shhh..." And like flipping a switch, Gwen's thunder was gone, and the humming, peaceful quiet of Cora and Sean's presence returned.

Still keeping his eyes on the Brandons, Sean's chin lowered. "Guys?"

"Yep! Gotcha!" one of them chirped. He looked over at Gwen. "Sorry, boss! We almost made it this time!" He turned to the other Brandon. "We gotta skedaddle."

"Oh yeah."

And just like that, they winked out of sight.

Gwen huffed a snort and folded her arms, eyeing Sean with a clever smile.

"Speak," he said.

"What are you gonna do?" she said with a light laugh. "What *can* you do?" Patting her chest, she continued, "This monkey sister of yours is entirely under *my* dominion. Attack me, you attack her, and she's truly the innocent in all this. Come at me, and I'll shred that soul of hers before you can do a damned thing, and you know it." She looked to the horizon. "I think that countdown's going. So let's all sit back and enjoy the show, shall we?" She tilted her head at Sean. "At least her soul would survive, right?"

"You destroy her soul, and your own essence will cease, Garamod," Sean said.

"You may be right." Gwen shrugged. "I very well might… but so will *your monkey sister*! Do you want to take that risk?"

Sean clenched and unclenched his fists.

Cora put her hand on his shoulder. "Peace, Sean. Be at peace…" She turned to me. "There's another way…"

Sean turned to me. He looked at me with such sadness and regret. And love? In his eyes, I felt my universe expand. In his gaze were all of the love songs I heard as a teenager that made me goosepimply, the poetry of Shakespeare, and the best romance novels I ever read.

Just from a look. If the new Cora was a vision, the new Sean was beyond words. I shivered under his gaze. "You're in love with me!" I gasped.

He nodded as we held one another's eyes. "Of course I am. But you have work to do. You're the only one who can stop this."

"Oh no you don't!" Gwen/Garamod snarled. "Don't you even dare!"

I knew what Sean meant, so I laid back onto the ground. I took three deep breaths, blocking out Gwen's furious words of rage. With each breath, I got closer and closer to where I needed to be.

Pop.

I was immediately above them. Gwen was looking at me with an expression of absolute hatred. I rose higher and higher, watching them shrink below me.

I turned and shot out once more to the canyon where the missiles were located.

It was getting easier and easier each time. I left my body with almost no effort at all, and almost as quick as the thought itself, the canyon lay below me. I descended down through the crevice at the top, down, down and down to the third missile. It had risen out of the silo, attached to a steel gantry. It reminded me of those old films of the moon launches—the rocket tethered by hoses and cables to a vertical steel strut. A mist of gasses were escaping from valves on the side, and the area echoed with a voice over a loudspeaker doing what I could only assume to be a countdown.

I was alone this time, but recalled Shaniqua's counsel from the last visit. I hovered over the missile, peering at its outer shell.

You misguided creation, I thought. You could have been a farm tractor, or an operating room… even an entire hospital! The money and effort spent bringing you into being could have been spent on life, not death…

Just as before, the metallic shape in front of me began to shimmer; but this time it was the entire missile, not just the warhead. I was making headway. Encouraged, I returned to my litany.

"*ENOUGH!*" blared in my mind. What the hell?

As if I had been grabbed by my scalp, the scene below

me spun in circles. The walls of the canyon whipped past me as I was flung around and around. I felt no pain, but was completely disoriented as I was flung straight up into the air, far above the canyon.

I was spinning from the force of what had launched me. Holding out my arms, I tried to steady myself.

"*NOT THIS TIME, MEATBAG!*" screamed with a bellowing shrillness in my mind.

I looked around me, but saw nothing!

Again I was grasped; this time my whole being was whipped around and around, a pressure on my spirit was crushing me!

I couldn't see my enemy, but I knew who… or *what* was doing this.

I forced my arms from my sides. With every fiber in my soul, I cried out.

GARAMOD! I REBUKE YOU! The pressure eased for a split second, and I managed to escape its grasp. I looked around to see it.

A spinning, formless mass of black and purple loomed over me, blotting out everything else.

I remembered Nana's lesson—knowing the demon's name took away its power. It needed to hide its true self always, and its name was, since time itself began, since the inception of evil, the key to overcoming it.

GARAMOD! I called out again. *I rebuke you! Leave this realm!*

I'LL TAKE YOU WITH ME! YOU AND ALL YOU LOVE!

The roiling stench of evil fell on me. With an evil howl of joy, it shot talons through me. I looked down at my chest, seeing bony talons, dripping with my blood and flesh spearing out of my torso. It had stabbed me from behind!

The pain... the pain was a sharp burn. Each of Garamod's claws writhed, with my entrails dripping from it. I was rent from my collarbone to my waist.

My soul, my deepest essence was being rent in half. I stared down, filled with terror and revulsion at my...my *self*!

YOUR BLOOD IN MY FIST! BLEED FOR ME, MEATBAG!

It opened its talons, spreading them wide, and I felt my ribs and spine crack. Blood filled my mouth, spilling over my lips and drenching my chest, rolling down onto the bony claw that was shoved out from me. I watched in agony as it shook its claws again.

RELENT OR I'LL BLEED YOU FOREVER KEIRA! YOU'LL BLEED FOR ME FOR ALL TIME!

I gasped, blood splattering out from my mouth.

I closed my eyes and felt tears sting.

So be it.

Very well, I gasped. *So it shall be...*

My head dropped as I resigned myself. Through the pain was terror of what was to come.

No.

I won't be afraid.

Not now. I lifted my head, and opened my mouth:

> *I will not be afraid*
> *Fear is the soul destroyer*
> *And would consume me*
> *Were I to allow it*
> *I rebuke fear*
> *To its face of many masks I stare*
> *unafraid*

One by one, I will watch those masks
fall away
Crumble to ash
And drift away
In the breeze of my love
Leaving nothing by myself
And I will still stand
Alone and unafraid.

The agony in me lessened.
SHUT UP MEATBAG!
I began the litany again:

I will not be afraid!

The claw wrenched me from side to side, breaking my back, and folding me over. The agony reached exquisite proportions, overloading my senses in a muddy cascade of pain as I was flung back and forth; my blood spewing from me in a fine mist.

I'LL BE FEASTING ON YOUR SOUL FOR A THOUSAND YEARS, WRETCH! Garamod's voice was guttural in my mind. I'LL FLAY YOU STRIP BY STRIP, FEASTING ON YOUR AGONY!

I bore down:

I rebuke fear!

I cried out through the pain and terror.
I rebuke YOU Garamod!
I continued the litany:

To its face of many masks I stare
unafraid
I rebuke fear

To its face of many masks I stare
unafraid

Knowing you don't have a clue is a power in itself. Knowing that I didn't know what was to come, that's what gave me the strength to go on... I drew a breath, and cried out:

One by one, I will watch those masks
fall away
Crumble to ash
And drift away!

I felt Garamod weaken. The thrusting blasts stopped, and I hung there in the air, still surrounded by that formless evil mist. I drew another breath, but before I spoke, my hands dropped to its talons, covering their scaly, putrid essence with my own, now bloody, dripping hands:

And drift away
In the breeze of my love

I straightened up.

Like the missile below me, Garamod only knew hatred, anger and the power of evil.

In the breeze of my LOVE, Garamod. I rebuke you... I stroked the surface of the talons, watching them fade away.

With a groan of the ages, Garamod faded. The pulsating, roiling cloud thinned. I watched as my figure undulated and sorted itself back into its previous form. The blood vanished, the rips in my body and clothing disappeared, and just like in my litany...

Leaving nothing by myself
And I will still stand

Alone and unafraid.

I floated alone again over the canyon.

I looked down to the missile. It still stood.

I sighed and descended to it.

Again, alarms were blaring. Before I had been hijacked by Garamod, I had made some headway with this missile's destruction, but not enough. They had tried to launch it, but now it was trembling and shaking. Flames were billowing out from cracks along the side I had created. If I left it as it was, the rocket's fuel would explode, wiping out every living thing in the canyon.

No.

I held my hands up to the rocket.

No... I said with my soul. *No more death. No more pain. Your time here is over…*

The silken, golden threads appeared on its surface. They pulsed and spread throughout the entire fuselage. From the tail to the nose cone, it was as if gossamer, golden netting had been draped over its entire length.

The flames stopped all at once.

And with a shudder and whooshing sound, the missile crumbled into dust. The pile fell, cascading over the pad and down into the silo below.

The alarms ceased.

I looked around me at the huge cavernous space.

It was finished.

Thirty Six

I POPPED BACK INTO MYSELF, rising to my elbows to find the human versions of Sean and Cora before me. I blinked at them.

"That really happened, didn't it?" I said.

Cora nodded silently at me. I looked sideways at the now smoldering remains of the Sanctuary, the smell of the fire still wafting in the air. Yes, yes it did. Such wanton destruction of this old building. What a waste.

I looked over beside me. Gwen, Roy, Shaniqua and Astrid were all laid out on the grass lawn, face up, sleeping soundly.

"Is Gwen all right?" I asked in a small voice.

"Yeah," said Sean. "Garamod had to leave her in order to pursue you into the Astral Plane." He looked around the area. "He's gone now, isn't he?"

"Yeah. I rebuked him and he faded away." I rubbed my

stomach. That sounded a lot easier than it had been. The memory of what that demon had put me through, that indescribable pain, the shock and horror of that episode would be with me for the rest of my life. But so would my victory.

Cora nodded. "He had his chance—"

"Again," added Sean.

"And this time he failed."

Sean sighed. "Yeah, thank goodness. This one would have been a lot worse than the last time. It was close, though."

"The *last* time?" I said.

Sean nodded. "Garamod had a real streak in the twentieth century. He was behind the start of World War I and then right behind it, World War II." He looked so sad. "He took advantage of a swell of hatred, ignorance, fear and greed that lasted thirty years…"

Cora put her hand on his arm. "From nineteen fourteen to nineteen forty-five, over a hundred million people died from wars." She stared at her feet and in a wistful voice added, "Not to mention the hundreds of millions of people maimed and traumatized. Mothers lost sons, children lost parents… thirty years of horror."

Sean looked around the meadow. "This one would have killed billions, Keira. *Billions.*" He drew in a breath. "Those are the stakes now."

Cora patted his arm. "They're learning, Sean."

"Yeah." He let out a huff of air. "But this was really close…"

"But we stopped it, right?" She had the sweetest smile. So what? She's a freaking angel, okay?

He nodded. "Yeah. And Garamod won't be back for

quite some time…"

"If ever," Cora added.

"*Really?*" I said.

She nodded. "When he fails, he takes a looong time licking his wounds. And…" she patted Sean's arm again. "With how much humanity's… well, *matured* since his last victory…" she smiled, and I could see that angelic radiance in her face when she did. It was full of such hope, beauty and joy… "I think humanity won't be as easy pickings for him anymore."

"So now what?" I said.

"We get back to our lives of course!" She patted herself. "There's still some years left in this form, and the Indigos still need me."

"What… you're not going back to…" I paused: oh what the hell. "Heaven?"

"It's not exactly like that," she replied. "When we enter your realm to live among you, we don't return to our original form until our human form passes away."

"Then you pass through The Veil."

She shook her head. "No. We're not moving from one stage to another; we're going home."

"Will we see you…" I pointed skyward. "Up there then?"

"Sort of… but it's different. I wish I could tell you more, but I'm unable to."

"But…"

Sean made a small wave. "No, Keira; that's how it is. Mysteries unfold and become revealed when the time is right." He stepped toward me and helped me to my feet. WOW! The pulse from him was awesome! It wasn't hard for my knees to go weak… and so he *did* bend over and help me up even more… Yummm…

Standing next to him I held his hand in mine, examining the palm. Nope; it looked like anyone else's hand. No sparkles, or glow—just a guy's hand. I traced it with my finger. "So you're an angel."

"Yep. I took my human form…"

"Why?"

He looked at me. "Because… I was asked to."

"By whom? God?"

"No… just leave it at that for now, okay?" He tilted my chin and kissed me.

Yes, it was wonderful. It was warm, sensuous, filled with desire… I mean *really* filled with desire! Oh man… the hubba hubba was going to be epic.

But.

I broke the kiss.

What's wrong? echoed in my head.

"You're kidding," I said out loud. "There are three people passed out on the ground!" That wasn't all of it, but that much was the truth. I turned to the others. "How do we go about waking them up?" I asked, stepping to Gwen. "Is she going to be all right?" I squatted down beside her, wiping a wisp of her hair from her face.

"Yeah. She'll have some memories, but they'll fade quickly…" Sean said, squatting down opposite me. "Like a dream."

"So… how do we wake her up? Is there some kind of angel thing you do or something?"

He snickered. "Nooo…" And nudged Gwen, whose eyelids fluttered open.

She gasped loudly and sat straight up. Her eyes were wide with terror. "Is he gone? Omigod, is he *gone*?" She looked around wildly.

"Yeah, sis. He's gone…" Sean said.

She threw her arms around him. "It was horrible! He—he—it started with like voices in my head, just crazy stupid thoughts about how this whole 'Veil thing' was a waste of time!" She looked past Sean to me.

"I thought they were *my* thoughts! And then… and then I became all fixated on how I really, *really* needed to marry Roy! He loves me right? But then…" She started crying. "Then I just got *weird*! I thought I was having a nervous breakdown or something, because I was… *watching* me do and say all sorts of crazy stuff!" She reached out to me. "I didn't *want* to leave The Sanctuary! I couldn't help myself!"

She stopped cold in her tracks, her eyes wide in terror. "I saw it! I saw that thing when I left and headed down the road! When I came upon Brandon and Brandon, I could *see* what was in meeee!" Her voice ended with that keen that went on and on.

"Hey!" Sean shook her. "GWEN!" His voice in that moment took on a tone and timbre that rolled over me as I watched. I saw a glow come off his back and run through his hands which gripped her shoulders. It was a golden aura that infused into her. "He's gone," Sean said, his voice still resounding with a power, but softly… If a sunrise over the ocean could say 'Good Morning!' it would be in that voice, I know it. "He's gone, and he'll never, ever be back…"

"Really?" Her voice wasn't small; it was skeptical. "Are you really sure?"

"Yeah, I am." The pulsing glow from Sean eased off.

"But I don't know which was him—*it*—and which was how I really am!"

"Yeah… he was a devious bastard," I said quietly as I

rubbed her shoulder.

"But it was all just me! They were *my* thoughts!"

Sean was still stroking her like a spooked, thoroughbred racehorse. "Only at the very start, Gwen... Once that beast got its toe in, it manipulated you more and more." His voice, now a calming tone said, "No, hon... they were temptations, that's all..."

"What the hell's that supposed to mean?" Gwen was wound up and wire tight. Her face, tight with confusion, stiffened in anger. "What the hell do you mean?"

He had squatted down next to her and pulled her to his shoulder like a child. "It means that we all have stupid thoughts sometimes, that's all. If we get tired, or upset, we think crazy things." Stroking her hair, he said, "Remember when you told me how much you hated me when we were kids, and I wouldn't let you come with me to the movies?"

It must have been something they had talked about ever since, because a smile sparked and Gwen buried her face in his chest. "I really wanted to see *Men In Black*! the commercials on TV were funny!"

"You were only seven, Gwen. I tried to tell you that you were too little for it... remember what you said?"

Her voice came out muffled. "That I hate you..."

"There were tons of times I hated you right back," he chuckled. "But we didn't really... we were pissed off, or hurt, and gave into temptation saying bad stuff, that's all." He pulled back a little, and looked at her tear-streaked face. "That demon latched onto you when you and Keira went into the Astral Plane. It waited there and fed every bad thought that crossed your mind since then. It grew in influence until it became strong enough and entwined enough with you to take over. It wasn't you."

"But…"

"Shhh… but *nothing*. You can't blame yourself, honey…" He stroked the side of her face.

"That would be like blaming someone who's house got broken into for having a nice house…" His voice gained an edge. "You were a victim of a master of lies."

Gwen's eyes widened for a moment. "Really?"

"Yeah… really. You're a wonderful person. An awesome sister!" He turned and looked at me. "And the greatest friend anyone could ever be blessed with, right?"

"Hell yeah!" I said, dropping down beside him. "The best friend!"

She looked from me back to Sean. "I said terrible stuff…" She looked at the embers of The Sanctuary. "I made that happen…" Her face went white. "Oh no! Roy!" She flung herself away from Sean and scrabbled across the grass to where he was.

"Roy! Roy! Wake up!" She was on her knees over him, poking at him. "Wake up, Roy!" She dropped her head to his chest. "He's breathing!" She looked up at me. "What did I dooooo?" Her face was wet with tears, and her hair, her beautiful hair lay snarled and straggled over her shoulders, all knotted and matted. "Help meeee!"

We were both at her side in a flash.

"He's okay, Gwen!" I said, giving her another shake. "He's just out from some smoke inhalation, that's all!" I snickered. "He's going to have one hell of a headache…"

And yes, as if on cue, Roy began to cough and sputter, his arms thrashing around. We backed away a little to give him room, and he sat right up and let go a loogie of black phlegm and mucus that sailed four feet. He hawked again, and spat once more.

Eeeww. Sorry, but c'mon; it was gross!

He wiped his mouth with his arm and looked around him. "Gwen!"

"Oh Roy!" She hugged him to her chest. "Oh baby! Oh Roy! I'm so sorryyyyy!"

Peeking up at us, Roy's eyes were wide in bewilderment. "Whaaa... wha happened?" he said, his voice muffled.

Looking past him, I saw that Cora was in the process of rousing Astrid and Shaniqua. I have no clue where she got them, but she had given each of them a bottle of water and was speaking gently.

Shaniqua stood, and they both helped Astrid to her feet. They were coming out of it a lot better than Roy, or Gwen for that matter. But dealing with the Indigos and paranormal events was just another day at the office for them I imagined. They stood together, watching us.

I called over to them. "Is there anything we can do here?" I asked, gesturing at the ruins behind me.

"No," Cora said simply.

"Then let's get out of here." I went over to the huge four by four that the two Brandons had rode out in. With three rows of seating, it could easily accommodate all of us.

Brandon and Brandon were so smugly confident they'd left the keys in the gi-normous Suburban. I checked the glove compartment while Sean fired it up to find a rental agreement made out to—get this— 'Brandon B. Brandon'—paid for with an Amex card.

I looked over my shoulder to Gwen. "Any idea why that demon had such a fixation on that name for his... *minions*?" I grinned, hoping she'd at least respond to the absurdity of it.

"No..." she said. "It really didn't let me in on the

reasoning." She *did* smile weakly though before she sidled up to Roy, who had an arm around her shoulders, holding her close.

"So now what?" I asked Sean. "Back to the hotel?"

He looked into the rearview mirror. "Any suggestions... er... 'Cora'?"

I looked back to her. She sat between Astrid and Shaniqua in the third row of seats. She closed her eyes for a moment.

Before I could say anything, Sean nudged me. "Don't mention anything about what you saw when the others were out cold, okay?" he whispered. "Let's just keep that to ourselves."

I gave him a quick nod. "You *do* have a driver's license, right?" I snickered.

"I get around okay," he quipped back.

"Why don't we just head to the airport?" Cora suggested. "Let's charter a plane and get back home." A huge smile lit her face. "Things are going to be working out quite nicely regarding this whole mess."

"What do you mean?" I asked.

"Well..." she looked from side to side. "I'm pretty sure that Kim Jong-Un is going to pretty much roll over and play nice. Those missiles crumbling to dust like they did really threw a scare into him."

"Yeah, but... an aircraft carrier exploded!" I said.

"That... is going to be blamed on a tragic accident. It seems that one of the cruise missiles on board spontaneously exploded and caused a chain reaction... there was no attack."

"All those sailors..." Gwen said.

Roy's voice had an edge. "No way! The States will have

to blame someone!"

"Oh, I suspect that there's a defense contractor that's in a lot of trouble."

"Really?" I said.

She nodded. "Yes. That tragedy really was an accident." She shook her head slowly. "The timing of it is astonishing, but it really was an accident."

Roy snorted. "Some accident. Five thousand people dead?" He tilted his head at Cora. "How can you be so sure?"

Sean spoke from the front seat. "Hey man, Cora's got unreal women's intuition, believe me."

Reaching over from her seat in the back, Cora put her hand on Roy's shoulder. "Fear not. There won't be a march off to war. Those people didn't die in vain. There's going to be a peace movement rising from this like the world has never seen."

"How the hell are you so damn sure?" Gwen said. It didn't take much for me to understand that she still didn't like Cora because of how I had been treated over Esther. I reached back from my seat in the front and patted Gwen's knee and nodded to her.

"It's okay, hon," I said. "Cora's not as bad as I thought." Now *that's* an understatement if ever there was one.

Gwen's lips pursed. "Still… how the hell could she be so sure?"

"Hey! I'm sittin' right here, y'know!" Cora said with a laugh. That broke the tension. She leaned over, her face next to Gwen's. "Let's just say, I have faith…" She shot me a look and nodded.

Thirty Seven

IT WAS NO BIG DEAL to find a charter at the airport which was willing to take us. The crises had come up so quickly the government hadn't set up any travel restrictions. Nobody *was* traveling yet, but there were plenty of companies still in Seoul who were willing to take on a last-minute charter. We were easily able to hire a Gulfstream large enough to accommodate us and do a one-way hop.

So eleven hours later, and a bunch of money lighter, we were taxiing on the runway in Spitzbergen, Norway.

Yeah, I figured that was the best place to head to first. Cora, Astrid, and Shaniqua wanted to be with the kids, plus Sean and Gwen's father was there along with my own parents.

And Esther was there.

I didn't know, nor didn't give a shit about Cora's opinion, nor her angelic powers. I was getting that girl back, come hell or high water. Yeah, there's a pun there, but I was determined as anything. More so now that the crises had passed.

Come on! I just saved the freaking world! I think I deserved some kind of prize or something, okay?

With nothing to declare, customs was a breeze, and the Illuminata had a van waiting for us when we came out of the small terminal. This time Gwen, Roy, Sean and I were relegated to the back while the Illuminata gang sat up front.

Cora turned from the shotgun seat beside the driver. "Normally, we have people wear hoods to keep our location on the island secret," she said.

"What! You made my parents wear hoods!" I snapped back through gritted teeth.

She burst out laughing. "Gotcha!" And settled back in her seat.

Astrid turned to me. "We'll be there very shortly, Keira."

My mouth opened and closed a couple of times. Sean patted my hand. "That was a good one," he said.

"Well…" I sat back in the bench seat. I wanted to grump at him, but… *it was a good one.*

We traveled up a roadway beside a fjord. I stared down the sheer cliffs on either side to the shimmering blue water flowing below. It was absolutely beautiful. I realized just then, with all the money I had, how little of the world I had actually seen.

"It's quite the view, isn't it?" Astrid said. Her chin began to tremble. "It's even more so now, for me… when Shaniqua and I left here to go meet you, we were both crying because we thought we'd never see it again." She reached over the back of the seat to me. "Thank you, Keira."

"I…" Okay, I started crying too. Guys don't get this—when it's a big deal, women cry. And for Pete's sake, avoiding a nuclear war… that's a big deal, right?

Right?

On our side of the fjord was a towering mountain. Eventually we came to a side road and turned in. That road led to a huge cave and when we pulled inside, a massive steel door, like a door to a bank vault, but as high as a house gaped open, while a corridor sloping downward began. We parked the van and got into an electric-powered tram like they have at Disney World. It began to descend down the tunnel carved out of solid rock.

"You guys are *under* the mountain?" I said to Cora.

She nodded. "The mass of the mountain would absorb the blast, and also the fallout. When we come to a stop we'll be two hundred feet below sea level."

"Glad I don't have claustrophobia," I said.

"Yes… that wouldn't be too good here, I think," she said. Again with that gentle smile.

Well, the corridor went in a spiral, down and down. The walls were finished in concrete, and so were quite smooth. It was pretty brightly lit from above, not your typical 'mountain lair' from the movies. We finally pulled into an atrium; I looked up and the ceiling must have been thirty feet above me. Warm lighting lit up an area the size of soccer field. It *was* an indoor soccer field, right down to the Astroturf grass.

A very, very crowded soccer field. It was packed with young people of all ages and races, and adults were sprinkled throughout the throng. It was as if a combined high school and elementary school was in session.

A boisterous cheer filled the space, rolling over us, with screams of joy and welcome. On and on it went, and then from a sound system, a swelling melody of victory and joy blared.

Holy shit!

Right on cue the crowd began screaming: "KEIRAAAA! GWENNN! ROYYY! AAAAS-TRIIID! SHAN-EEE-QUAAA!" In a rousing cheer, our names became a chant that sent thrills to my toes.

"They're playing your tune, girl!" Sean said.

He jumped out, and holding my hand, led me from the tram onto the ground.

I thought the cheer was loud, but when my feet hit the ground, it doubled in volume and excitement. I waved to the crowd with both hands.

Mom and Dad ran to me, threading through the throng. Dad picked me up and spun me in a circle before letting me down. Together, the three of us held each other.

Yeah, Mom was all crying and sniffling, which was a good thing, because I was too. Dad just pressed both of us to himself, rubbing his hands over our shoulders to beat the band. If he kept it up, I'm sure my clothes would have burst into flame.

Off to the side, Devon and Buster had come from the crowd and were gathered around Roy, Sean and Gwen.

I couldn't see Astrid nor Shaniqua, because they were completely engulfed by the rest of the girls who had surged forth to welcome their own heroines back in victory.

Mom, Dad and I continued our embrace until my arms were about to fall off. We relaxed our 'life grip' on each other and stepped away with me looking at them. Mom wouldn't stop patting my face.

"If your Nana was here, Keira, she'd shit herself!" she said.

"Mom!" I burst out laughing.

I looked over at the Indigo crowd. Just as I was about to ask, a blond, fourteen-year-old girl shoved her way through the crowd and ran at me full tilt.

Esther!

With blond hair streaming behind her, she leapt up at the last second. She scissored her legs around my waist and took my head into a bear hug embrace.

"You did it!" she said. "You guys really, really did it!"

A year and a half ago my great aspiration was to become a famous celebrity. I enrolled in acting school not because I wanted to bring life to a well-crafted script and expand people's appreciation of their lives through my mastery of a difficult craft. No, I just wanted to be a famous celebrity; adored by thousands and have people point at me on the street.

As I held Esther, I was flabbergasted by how much I'd changed. A year and a half ago I was as shallow as a saucer of milk set out for a kitten. And now, having been instrumental in preventing Armageddon, all I felt was joy and gratitude that all these people around me... everyone in the world, actually, could just go about their lives.

We were all aboard this pale, blue dot floating in space. Every day people will be born, and people will die. Some will fall in love, others will fall out of love. The world will turn, and life would go on.

I held Esther tightly, remembering Sean's words about how close a call we had.

I didn't feel *too* proud. In fact, in that moment, I closed my eyes, and said out loud to whoever was listening, "Thank you."

"What are you thanking me for, silly?" Esther said with a laugh. "You're the one who saved the freaking world!" She pulled her face from my neck and looked at me, her eyebrows a pair of question marks.

"I'm grateful we're all here," I said, looking around the atrium. "And that we can all go back home." I relaxed my grip, and she slid down to the floor.

She pulled at my hand. "Come on! All the kids from The Abbey are here!"

I let her guide me over to the edge of the crowd to see the group of girls from Ireland. I spent a fair chunk of time there. At first it was a place of refuge for me; it then became a place close to my heart.

They were all there. Sophie, Irina and Noor were off to one side, their hands on little Mary Jane's shoulders. She was smiling at me and waving.

"You lost a tooth, Mary Jane!" I dropped to my knees and hugged her. Mary Jane was the smallest and youngest of the bunch.

Behind us an exasperated voice exclaimed, "She didn't *lose* it; her gums matured to the degree where the roots of her deciduous teeth could no longer be sustained by them!"

I spun around to see my favorite twelve-year-old on the planet looking at me through owl-sized eyeglasses. I shook my head and held out an arm. "Rita Mosquita'… look who's growing up!"

"Yes, well, biology is a powerful force, no doubt," she said, suddenly shy. It had been just a few weeks since I last saw the kids at The Abbey, and yet, I could see how quickly they were all growing. She gave me a hug, and whispered in my ear, "I was really, really scared, Keira!" clenching me tightly.

Rita was the most powerful of The Abbey kids in terms of paranormal abilities. She had demonstrated a phenomenal degree of telekinetic power in defeating my grandfather David Holmes when he had all of us under the barrel of a gun. And yet, despite this, she was still a twelve-year-old girl. I held her. "We all were. And it's all over."

"Yes..." she said. She pulled away and looked serious again. "But those people from Blackwatch are still somewhat of a threat. The Illuminata want all of us to remain here until they can determine the nature of that organization." Oh, and I need to also mention she had, by far, the highest IQ of anyone I knew—even Gwen.

I nodded. I was pretty sure they were part of Garamod's plot, but I wouldn't bet my life on it. According to Cora, Blackwatch had been trying to find the Indigo children for some time. They saw the children as potentially powerful weapons. Their connection to David Holmes, and subsequently Garamod was open to question.

"Well, I don't know about you, but I can't wait for us to get back home." I turned to Esther. "How about you, hon? I got a room all ready for you in Kingston."

"Yeah..." she said, biting her lip as she looked away.

What the hell? I gave her a nudge. "What do you mean 'yeah'?"

She looked up at me. Fourteen years old and full of fire and fury when she wanted to, looked back shyly. "Well... I've been thinking about that."

I'll admit that I wanted to read her mind, but I didn't because Esther had a similar gift, and I was pretty sure she'd sense me poking around.

Before I could pursue the issue, Mom and Dad joined us.

"There's a reception, Keira, and you're the guest of honor," she said. She and Dad looked so proud they looked like they'd explode any minute.

So together, Esther and I, along with Mom and Dad went to the massive dining hall that was all decked out in bunting and flowers for a celebration. It struck me that this was probably the only celebration on the entire planet for what had happened.

I don't know why, but that felt right to me.

It was a buffet-style meal, and because of the reach across continents and cultures the variety of dishes on the smorgasbord was incredible. Curry dishes from India, incredible New York style pizza, fondues from Scandinavia and an unbelievably tasty series of dishes from the heart of Africa were just a few of the offerings. I sampled delicacies that had names I could barely pronounce, and stuffed myself.

There was also dancing and plenty of booze. I had my fair share of gimlets, let me tell you. But I also danced my legs off.

It had been a long, long time since I had been dancing. I danced with Dad, Esther, Roy, and even Gwen.

It was a blast. A combination rave and PTA soiree with all the kids running around.

Later in the evening as things were beginning to wind down, Esther tugged at my sleeve while I was chatting with Astrid and Shaniqua and the other adults from The Abbey.

"I want to talk to you about something," she said. "Privately?"

"Sure!" I made my excuses and followed her into one of

the corridors. It was where they had classrooms set up. She took me all the way down to the library. It was a pretty good size, filled with old leather chairs and couches and long oak tables.

"So, have you decided where our first vacay's gonna be?" I asked. "Skiing in Chile, or do you want to go to Disney World?" I knew that at the age of fourteen Disney World would seem kind of childish for her, but I remember having a blast there with my parents when I was fifteen!

"Yeah, those sound like good ideas..." she said. She sat at one of the reading tables and patted the seat beside her. "But with all the running around getting here and stuff, I'm worried that I'll be falling behind in my studies..." Her voice faded.

An invasion of butterflies, whapped and whirred in my stomach, knowing something big was coming...something I probably wouldn't like. "No biggie," I said. My voice was high. It always got high pitched when I got nervous. "We'll just get you a private teacher or something." I sat down beside her. "Actually, maybe we can hire someone away from a Montessori School. I went to one when I was your age for a while and it was pretty good."

"Yeah..." She stared down at the tabletop. "Maybe..."

"Maybe. *Maybe*?" I leaned forward. "What do you mean 'Maybe'?" The butterflies had grouped together in my gut forming a ball of ice. Oh no...

Esther looked sad. Grief-stricken, actually. Like she had just lost her best friend, and it was my fault.

Before she could say anything, I asked, "Hey, what's going on?"

She set her chin. I knew that look; when I had stayed at The Abbey, and before Esther and I became close, we started off as adversaries. She thought I was some interloper rich kid who was just playing around in the world of paranormal experiences, and I thought she was a young teen who was way too big for her britches.

But during my time there I got to see another side of her. Esther was at The Abbey because her family was frightened of her ability to read minds. They gave legal custody of her to the Illuminata because they didn't know what to do. Nevertheless, in a way, they rejected her when she was still a little girl. That gave her a chip on her shoulder, and made it hard for her to fit in.

When I was growing up, I too had always felt like I was on the outside looking in. We both learned that our sense of alienation from the rest of the world was something we had in common. That opened the door for us to get to know one another, and we found we had more in common than differences.

I grew to love Esther dearly. I knew I had the money to give her anything in the world she needed, and the idea of becoming her legal guardian was planted in my heart as well as my mind. There was opposition to this on the part of the Illuminata, and they had been unwilling to relinquish custody to me.

I developed one big chip on my shoulder as I tried to fight them.

But now... the look Esther was giving me...

"Hey..." I said. "You pissed off at me?"

"No!" she said.

"You sure look it right now." Her chin was set, and her eyes were dark under knitted brows.

"I'm not angry, I'm scared!" she spat out. Her hands on top of the table rolled, and her fingers were knotted together so tightly her knuckles were white.

"What are you afraid of?" I said, keeping my voice as gentle as possible.

"That... that you're gonna hate me."

My head rocked back like I had been slapped. "What the hell are you talking about? I love you!"

She shook her head slightly from side to side. "No, you won't." Her lips curved down in an upside down U shape. "You're gonna hate me because I don't want to come live with you."

My jaw dropped. "Whaat?"

"I've been thinking about it, and I'd been talking to Rita Mosquita' about it too," she said in a rush. "I couldn't ask any of the grown-ups here because they're all Illuminata and would stick together!"

"Rita! What the hell did she say about me?" I thought that Rita liked me!

"She didn't *say* anything! She... she asked me a question..."

"Oh? Like what?"

"She asked me how old you were."

"I'm twenty-four."

Esther nodded. "Yeah, you're ten years older than me." She looked away. "And that got me thinking on my own."

"What else did Rita ask you?"

She turned back to me. "Nothing. She said she wanted *me* to think about that kind of stuff on my own. She said that I was smart enough to figure out the rest."

"What did you *figure out?*" Yeah, my voice got sharp.

"I wondered how much experience you had with dealing with younger kids."

"Well..."

She leaned forward. "None," she said. "You're an only child."

"Well, I went to school! There were younger kids at school!"

"Did you ever hang out with them?"

"Nooo…" I clutched at a straw. "But I went to summer camp a bunch of times too! We all lived in bunkhouses!"

"You went to summer camp, but you were never a counselor." She held up her hand. "I know because I asked your mom."

"But Esther…"

"Keira…" She held her arms out, gesturing at the surroundings. "Since I was six years old, all I've ever known is being a ward of the Illuminata! You grew up with your parents and all that stuff! I love you! I really do!"

My eyes started to burn. "There's a 'but' coming, isn't there?"

"But we're from two different worlds, Keira! And I'm gonna be fifteen years old! I'm gonna move to a new home, leave the life I had, and… start all over again?"

"But Esther!"

She held up a hand. "You know I'm right."

I burst into tears.

Because she was.

Thirty Eight

THERE REALLY WASN'T ANY REASON FOR ME TO STICK AROUND NORWAY. I figured that Blackwatch, just like Brandon and Brandon, melted from our world when Garamod was defeated. But the Illuminata had a lot more at stake; the welfare of hundreds of children depended on them, and they would err on the side of caution.

Including Esther's welfare.

Since meeting my Nana, I've dealt with sprits and their grief. I thought that when Nana passed on I knew all about the pain of loss.

I had barely scratched the surface.

Leaving Esther behind in Norway was the second hardest thing I had ever done in my life. I made a good show of it for her sake, though. I kept my mind blocked to hers, and nor did I attempt to read her thoughts. Sometimes... sometimes it's better to keep a distance from people you love, right?

My decision to leave quickly was finalized when I went to Mom the following morning. I had planned to tell her about what had happened, cry on her shoulder and see if she could come up with some way I could weasel Esther into changing her mind.

Fat chance.

When I told Mom about what had gone on between Esther and I the night before, she nodded sadly.

"I was afraid this was going to happen," she said.

"What? You knew? She told you?" I was floored! "You two talked about me?" My temper spiked about a million degrees.

"Hell no!" Mom threw up both hands at me, palms out. "Esther didn't ask my opinion about anything!"

My eyes narrowed. "Well then, *what exactly* did you guys discuss that made you 'afraid this was going to happen'?"

"She asked if you had ever looked after little kids when you were growing up. Like babysitting and stuff like that."

"Oh." I had never, ever babysat. First of all, parents in our social circle had live-in nannies for the most part. But... I'll admit it now, the idea of looking after little kids had never really been anything I was interested in.

Mom held a hand out to me. "I got the feeling Esther was having some second thoughts, Keira. And maybe I was being a chicken, but I gave her a wide berth. Because if things turned out poorly for you regarding her I didn't want to be on the wrong side."

"Wrong side?"

She looked thoughtful. "Yes. I wanted to be the person you could come to... not a person to blame."

"Mom... do you think Esther's right?"

She blinked at me a few times. "Right? You guys are going to be seeing each other anyway, right? You're taking her to Disney World next month, correct?"

"Yeah." After the discussion last night, it took Esther a fair bit of time to get me to understand —because I kept blubbering like a baby—that she wasn't cutting me out of her life; she was just putting our relationship into a better place. "Yeah," I said again, "we're going to Disney World... and next year I'm taking her skiing..." My head jerked up. "Wait a minute! You didn't answer the question!"

"Huh?" Mom looked at me innocently.

"I was asking if you thought Esther made the right call in not letting me adopt her." I nodded slowly. "That was a pretty good deflection, though." I leaned forward. "Do you think she's right? That I *shouldn't* adopt her?"

Mom just looked at me silently. I threw up my hands in surrender.

Damn.

***

So I corralled Gwen and Roy to make arrangements to get back to Kingston.

"You feel like flying, Roy?" I asked.

"Not this time."

Great. Another charter on my Amex card.

One thing they don't tell you about when it comes to saving the world and you're a zillionaire—that shit costs *real money*.

When Roy booked the charter flight, Gwen found Sean in the library going through old manuscripts and papers the

Illuminata had decided were important enough to want to save the originals, and gave him a heads-up.

We said our goodbyes to everyone. I even told Cora Gaines that she was smarter about Esther's welfare and prospects than I was.

"She's going to have a happy, wonderful, and fulfilling life, Keira," she said. "And you're going to be playing a major role in it."

My voice became a whisper. "Is that your honest to angel truth? Did you do some peeking into the future?"

She just blinked innocently and smiled. "I've never lied to you, have I?"

We boarded our plane—a Lear this time—and settled in. Roy and Gwen sat side by side, and Sean plopped into the seat beside me. He took my hand in his, and that old magic happened again. A sense of warmth and comfort blossomed up my arm, filling me with a sense of peace and joy.

I held his hand all the way back home. Below us, the Atlantic Ocean whizzed by as my thumb and index finger traced over and around his hand. I wanted to remember every trace of his touch, every twinge of that energy that passed between us. I wanted the memory to be burned into my brain to last me a lifetime.

Leaving Esther behind in Norway was the second hardest thing I had ever done in my life. I knew when we landed that I was going to do the hardest thing.

Thirty Nine

W HEN WE LANDED AT KINGSTON we had to take a taxi home. It was big enough to accommodate all of us but I let Gwen, Roy and Sean take the backseat and hopped in the front.

"Where to, hon?" he asked.

"What the hell?" I said. "You got a New York accent!" I stared over at him wide-eyed.

"Born and bred in the Bronx, baby!" he replied with a cheesy grin. "And a dollar to a donut you grew up on the East Side, right?"

"Sixty-eighth and Second!" I replied.

He held out his hand, "They call me 'Cowboy.' Why, I'll never figure out. I think I've been on a horse maybe three times or something. But once you get a nickname, it's all over."

As he drove us through downtown Kingston and over the causeway bridge Cowboy kept up a patter of his life story. He came to Canada thirty-five years ago, raised his kids and was easing himself into semi-retirement.

"So whaddya doin' up here in K-town?" he asked me. "Visiting?"

I gave it a thought. "I inherited a house, fell in love with the area, and I think I'm going to settle here," I said.

"It's a great burg, Keira," he said. "You could do a lot worse, and I don't think you could do much better." He eyed the passengers in the back. "You two guys—you grew up here; I've seen ya's around." He gave a quick nod to Gwen. "You used to deliver mail, am I right?"

She nodded smiling. "Yuppers. Now I work for Keira."

"Oh yeah?" He turned to me. "Whaddya do?"

"When I'm not saving the world, I convince ghosts to go to heaven," I replied without missing a beat.

Cowboy barked out a laugh. "Okay! Okay! I get it! Look doll, I'm a big boy, awright? You could just say, 'none-a-ya's biznezz.'" He tapped the steering wheel, still chuckling. "But I gotta tell you, that's a good one."

He continued to regale us with stories and anecdotes the rest of the way home. I had no idea that taxi drivers led such interesting lives.

"Drop Roy and I off at Dad's will you, Keira?" Gwen said.

It was just a short run down the road between Gwen's father's house and mine. Devon and Buster would be coming back from Norway in a few days. But for now he and my parents wanted to stay for a while with the Indigos and their group. It seemed the Illuminata had grown on them.

"Bless you, sis," Sean said. He turned to me and wiggled his eyebrows when they got out and made their goodbyes.

I chewed on the inside of my cheek until we got out of the cab.

He took my hand, and again I felt that energy spark between us. Oh man, it was niiiice.

But.

I shook his hand off.

He stared at me. "Keira… what's going on?"

"Let's go around back to the dock," I said.

"No," he replied. We were standing in the driveway. "You got something to say. I don't need to read your mind to know that it's not going to be good news." He folded his arms and stared at me. "Is this about Cora Gaines?"

Shaking my head I replied, "No." I darted my eyes up into his. "You guys *do* love one another, but you're not *in love*, right?" When he nodded, I said, "She's more like a sister to you."

"Yeah…that's a good analogy. I think the world of her, but we're not mates."

"Angels have mates?" This was getting interesting.

"In very rare circumstances, yeah."

"Do you have a mate?" I pointed my finger at the sky. "I mean…up there?"

He looked up. "It's not really like that, but I know what you mean." He dropped his eyes back to mine. "And no, I don't have one 'up there'."

He took another step towards me, and I backed away again, holding my palm out toward him.

His face fell and he sighed. "Say what you need to say."

So this was it. I shuffled my feet, crunching the gravel of

the driveway. In the movies, we should be standing on a windswept airport runway in the rain like in Casablanca. Or maybe on a train platform with steam rising and the conductor hollering, 'All aboard!' But no, we were just standing outside my house.

"I love you," I said. "I think I fell in love with you the first time I saw you and you scowled at me."

He snorted. "Yeah, I did, didn't I?" Holding up his hand, he added, "In my own defense, I scowled because I was astonished with how smitten I was with you from the beginning. That kind of thing doesn't happen to me and I was... well, kind of confused, to tell you the truth."

When he took a step toward me with his hands outstretched I skittered backward.

"Keira?"

I took a breath. "Back in Norway, Esther told me that she and I were from two different worlds; the things that separated us was a chasm too deep for us to bridge at this time in her life."

"Yeah," he said. "I'm sorry, because you really love that kid." He made a small shrug. "But... y'know... maybe she's right?"

"Of course she's right Asshat!" I pointed at him. "The boundary between you and I is a million times wider!"

He blinked in surprise and confusion. "Whaaat?"

"At least Esther's human!"

"Hey! I was born! Just like you!"

"You have memories from before that, right?" He nodded. "Good grief, Sean! You're an angel!" I waved my hands at him. "I live my life day by day, and you... you *don't*." I shook my head slowly from side to side. "I don't know how much stuff you know... I can't even fathom what it must be like to be the way you are…"

"Let me show you!" he pleaded. He held his hands out to me. "I can show you the universe! I can take you to places you've never dreamed of!"

"You could do that…"

"Yes!"

I dropped my head, shaking it. "You don't get it, Sean. We're supposed to discover stuff like that *together*. There's nothing… in this world, or out there you don't know about, is there?"

"That's right. And I want *you* to see it!"

I kept my head down and began to sing softly:

> *I was dumbfounded by truth*
> *You cut through lies*
> *I saw the rain dirty valley…*
> *You saw Brigadoon!*
> *I saw the crescent…*

I lifted my head to look at him through my tears.

> *You saw the whole of the moon*

"Isn't that right, Sean?"

His face took on an expression of understanding. His eyes focused on me and he nodded. "Yes," he said. "I do."

I stepped forward and gently cupped his face. I kissed him briefly, and without looking back walked up the driveway to my home.

And my life alone.

***

I really ought to end this story here. Because if I did, you'd have a taste of how empty my life became in that moment.

That was the saddest... no, that word's too gentle. That was a crucially barren experience. My heart and soul were wind-scoured rocks on a desert plain, resting on dry, cracked, soil bereft of all life.

As I was bereft of the promise of joy in mine.

Forty

LIFE GOES ON. I wasn't inside the house for a minute—I didn't even have a chance for a good cry—when my phone rang. My jaw dropped as I stared at the Caller ID.

It was from my lawyer's office. As well as looking over my legal and financial affairs, Mr. Thompson was also responsible for filtering out cases for Gwen and I to work on regarding The Veil.

I answered and we went through the typical pleasantries. "What's up?" I finally asked.

"I have an assignment for you, Ms. Swanson."

I looked out the window of the living room down the driveway. Sean was gone. I turned back into the room. "Okay, what do you have for me?"

***

And that's how it went. Every few weeks, or few months, my phone would ring, I'd have a chat with Thompson, he'd send the details to Gwen via email, and the three of us would gallivant somewhere in the world to help a lost soul find its way home.

I broke down and bought a toy for Roy—an eight-passenger Lear that could go over the Atlantic, or even the Pacific, nonstop. It was *expensive*! But I have to admit it's a dynamite plane; we could get in and out of our assignments with even less hassle than ever.

One night we were in the private terminal at an airport in Austria waiting for Roy to file a flight plan. Gwen was wearing a smart suit with a skirt, and I was in a white top and yoga pants. A sense of déjà vu came over me, and I looked around the airport.

Gwen noticed. "What's the matter?" she asked.

I smiled. "Back when we first met, I had a premonition of you and I standing here."

"Really?" When I nodded, she added, "feels like a lifetime ago…"

"Yeah." I reached out and took her hand. We stood watching the runway as Roy steered our plane up to the gate.

The tradition of Key Lime pie after a transition was maintained.

And so life went on.

My parents wound up staying in Norway though. The Illuminata changed its structure somewhat after the scare and decided to keep The Sanctuary going even though peace had broken out all around the world. They asked Mom and Dad if they'd stay on as House Parents to a group of kids that were there. And guess which group? Yeah, the gang from The Abbey…including Esther.

Mom jumped at the chance, especially after hearing about Sean and I not working out.

"I got a bad feeling this is going to be as close to having grandkids that your father and I are going to get, Keira," she said.

I didn't argue the point. It was a little scary, but the truth of the matter is I had zero interest in meeting anyone. Something broke inside me when I ended it with Sean, and I didn't think it would ever heal.

Devon and Buster came home to Kingston, though. He missed his house and his wife's spirit rattling around in it. While he was a widower, he was far from lonely.

The trip to Norway had taken a toll on him, though. When we picked him up at the airport, he looked frailer than ever; his multiple sclerosis was raging through him. Looking at his aura I saw it had dwindled. It still had a beautiful series of colors, but they were faded.

"Devon…" I said. "You know there are clinics that can really help you." We were in his living room watching the Yankees and Blue Jays battle it out. It was the bottom of the seventh and tied up 4-4.

He waved his hand dismissively. "My time here will end when my time *here* ends. If there was one thing I realized over the pond, it's that this…" He waved at the room. "This is where I belong, okay?"

I didn't argue the point. Gwen and Roy had moved back into her old home so they could look after him.

After that flurry of cases, it's not surprising that we didn't have any more to work on after Devon returned. It was as if the universe took pity on us and gave Gwen a long stretch of being with her dad.

Before having to say goodbye.

I was in the sunroom of my home when Gwen walked in. Her face was tear-stained, and she was alone when I looked up at her.

"At least he didn't disappear on me the way your Nana did on you!" she said.

I stood up and held her as she cried.

"Where's Roy?"

She sniffled. "He and Sean are back at the house. They both figured that it would be best for me to come get you on my own…"

"Sean's there?"

She wiped her eyes and blew her nose. "Yeah. Dad phoned him two days ago to get up here right away. He's been at the house for a day or so…."

"So… your dad knew it was time…"

She nodded. "I think his spirit's still there, Keira. He was sitting in front of the TV when he passed away. His hand was petting Buster who was on the floor beside him…" She started to really cry hard. "And Buster won't leave him!"

"You want us to…?"

She nodded.

When we got to the house, Devon was still sitting in his easy chair. He looked asleep, not dead; instead of his head lolling back or his tongue hanging out, he simply had laid back and closed his eyes.

When I entered the room, Buster saw me and sat up, letting Devon's hand slide off the back of his neck.

But instead of scampering away at the sight of me, he let out a low wail that big dogs can do; a soft howl of grief.

He then stood and shook himself. Watching me, he

padded across the room and plopped down on his butt in front of me.

We stared at each other.

"Buster...?" I said.

He let out a soft "woof!" I reached out and for the first time in my life was able to pet a dog. We gazed into each other's eyes, enjoying the respite in this hour of sadness.

To this day he's never left my side.

Roy and Sean stood behind Devon's chair.

Roy kept wiping away tears. "He was such a good shit, you know that?" he said.

Sean blew his nose. "Yeah, he was, man; I'm glad you met him." I was surprised; I didn't think angels cried.

Between us and the guys, Devon's and Mary's spirits hovered. I don't know how it happened, but they were younger. Every time in the past, when I would see spirits, they would appear at the age they died. But not this time. Mary was wearing a white dress and Devon was in a snappy suit from the nineteen eighties. He gave me an impish grin as he brushed the front of his black, pinstripe three-piece number.

"You guys are wearing your wedding outfits, aren't you?" I said. They both nodded smiling. I'm not kidding; I think Mary laughed.

"You can see them!" Gwen said.

I nodded. "Take my hand," I said.

She reached out and took my hand, and in an instant, the shining whiteness of The Veil appeared.

"Mommy!" Gwen gasped. "Daddy!"

"Holy shit!" Sean said. He came out from behind the chair.

I watched as the four of them looked at each other. Sean

lifted his hand.

Don't do any angel shit Asshat! I yelled at him with my mind.

He flicked a glance at me. "Don't worry, Keira." He took his raised hand and glided it along the air where his mother's spirit was, his eyes wide in wonder. "I've missed you so much, Ma," he said. "I know it's dumb and stuff, but... I have..."

She raised herself on her tiptoes and brought her face to his cheek. Even though they were separated by two dimensions, she kissed the side of his face as best she could. Mary turned to Gwen and did the same.

Gwen felt it; her free hand went to the side of her face. She hung on to my hand with her other for dear life, though. She didn't want to chance breaking the moment by letting go of me.

"I love you so much, Mommy," she said, her voice small.

Mary nodded, smiling. Beside her, Devon looked as proud as a peacock watching his family's last moment of joy and love on this good Earth. He reached out and nudged Mary, who turned to him. Cocking his head at The Veil, he asked the question with his eyes, and she nodded.

They both turned to Roy and I. Mary blew me a kiss, and Devon gave him a thumbs-up. Just before he stepped through, he turned to me and mouthed, *Go Jays!*

And was gone.

Arrangements were all made, and the funeral took place. It was sad and bittersweet, joyful in memories, and heartfelt from beginning to end. Just as all good lives that come to a good end should be celebrated.

And Buster was by my side throughout.

I had to buy a king-sized bed, because he insists every

night to sleep at the foot. He follows me everywhere. Even when I take a shower, he's outside the bathroom door, waiting patiently for me to come back out. And when I do, his ears perk up as if he wants to say 'See! I knew you'd be back!'

I've always wanted a dog, and Buster's doing everything he can to make up for lost time.

We make a good team. Roy and Gwen got their own dog shortly after. Like Buster, she's a mutt too—part Lab, part collie, part any and everything. They got her from the Kingston Humane Society the same way Devon had gotten Buster.

We didn't get any assignments from Mr. Thompson for months and months after Devon passed away. Which was okay. It gave Roy and Gwen a chance to do some traveling together. They became real nerd travelers, too. They went to Latin America to visit the old Mayan temples, and then went to Europe to see some particle collider or something that was a big deal for people into physics.

They took a pass on the Eiffel Tower, can you believe that?

They were gone for almost two months, and just when they were coming home, I received some bad news. Gwen was going to be quitting.

And it was Sean who told me.

Forty One

I WAS IN THE SUNROOM READING the latest thriller adventure by Mark Dawson. Look, I'm all girly and stuff, okay? When I gussy up, I'm pretty hot, and I know it. I like lipstick and looove getting manicures and pedicures. BUT when I read for pure enjoyment, I read thrillers. You know, like James Bond novels and stuff like that. I read every single Jack Reacher book after I saw the Tom Cruise movie. Then I found the John Milton series by another guy from England, and not only have I read those, I *reread* them. The latest one had come out, and I was spending the afternoon in the sunroom with a pot of tea and enjoying the chase and adventure.

Until Buster started barking at the back door of the sunroom.

Buster never barks.

But he was up against the back door, yipping and yapping. There was something... *or someone* out there.

Buster's tail was wagging to beat the band, so I got up and went to the door and opened it. He bounded past me and flew yipping around the side of the house where Nana's rose garden was. I was right behind him.

I turned the corner to see Sean Jones on his knees, patting and rubbing Buster, who was wearing himself out licking and pawing at Sean in that doggy joy only those animals can do.

I stopped dead in my tracks.

"What are you doing here?" I said.

He got to his feet. Yes, he looked every bit as yummy as he did the first time I laid eyes on him. Those blue eyes were so gorgeous, and his smile was a lot warmer and friendlier than my brusque greeting.

"Hi, Keira!" he said. He came over to me.

"This really isn't fair, Sean. You just popped over angel-style, didn't you?" There was no sound of a car in the driveway; one minute I was reading a book on my Kindle, and the next minute, Buster was going berserk.

He shrugged. "Yeah, I did. I don't do it a lot, but I figured this was a good time to pull something like that."

"Why? Is the world coming to an end again?" I knew it wasn't. His aura was too bright and cheerful.

"Well..." He scuffed the grass with the toe of his shoe. "I'm a bringer of news..." He looked back up at me. "We angel types are good at bringing news, you know."

"Yeah, yeah..." Did he have the slightest idea how the sight of him broke my heart and made me happy all at the same time?

You're not the only one to feel that way, dummy! rang in my head. His mouth had such a smartass grin.

"Cut it out!" I crossed my arms and stamped my foot.

He held up his hands in mock surrender. "Okay, okay!" He lowered his hands. "I'm here to bring you tidings..."

"Tidings? You sound like it's Christmas or something!" Angels and tidings? I saw that Charley Brown Christmas show a million times.

"Well... it's *kind* of like that..." He took a breath. "Someone's going to be telling you tomorrow that she's having a baby..."

What? Who? Huh? My hand flew to my mouth. "Gwen? She's pregnant?"

He nodded. "Yeah. But she's kind of hesitant to tell you..."

"Why? That's great news!"

He drew in his breath. "Beeee-caawwzze... she's going to stop The Veil transitioning you two do."

"WHAT!"

But then it hit me—of course she would! Baby, nursing, diapers... shit, being pregnant and dealing with things that go bump in the night? Nooo... of course she would! Oh no... How would I continue?

"And I'm here to offer my services in her stead," he said.

"Oh Sean..." I reached out and hugged him.

And holy zowie ka-zowie... I had forgotten how the touch of him just went through me like the output from a nuclear reactor. Whoa! Every particle of oxygen left my body as we embraced.

"NO!" I sprang back from him. "You Asshat! That wasn't fair!"

He laughed. "That wasn't even me at full tilt!"

I jabbed at him with my finger. "You're still a goddamn angel, Sean! Not fair!"

He snorted. "Some choice of words there!"

"You know what I mean!"

He looked from side to side to make sure the coast was clear and then... well... pulsed or something. For a split second I saw him in his full nature, just like I did back at The Sanctuary in Korea. He's a beautiful specimen of a man, but he's something else entirely when he's in angel mode. My knees went weak.

"Cut that out!" I said, backing away.

"Okay, okay... I'm just messing with you."

I shook my head at him. "You're a real bastard, you know that? You know how I feel about this!" I jabbed myself with my thumb. "Me! Human!" I jabbed a finger at him. "You! Angel!" I shook my head. "No way, José. We'd be messing with stuff that shouldn't be messed with, and YOU KNOW IT! How different is that than what Garamod was doing to Gwen, huh?"

He nodded. "You do have a fair argument, Keira." But he was watching me with a cocked eyebrow. "I have more tidings."

"Oh?"

"Yeah." He rubbed the ground with his toe again, pausing. "Aww shit," he said. He lifted his head and looked at me. "There's a few billion girls on this planet, right?"

I nodded.

"And yet, in all of my 'angel-guy' stuff, I could have fallen in love with any of them. Hell, at any time in human history!"

"I know, I know!" I said with a wave. "Time's not the same for beings like you!" I shrugged. "So what's your point?"

"My point is that out of all the..." He made finger quotes. "Beings on this planet, why would it have to be you?"

My head jerked. "Did you just slag me?"

"No, dummy; I just asked you a question. What makes *you* all that so damn special, huh?"

I shrugged. "I dunno..."

He stepped up to me, holding me in his gaze. "It's beeee-caawwzze... Keira... my darling Keira... my sweet, Keira..."

He bent and kissed my forehead. "It's because you're an angel, too."

Forty Two

WHAAAT?

I didn't feel 'angel-y' or 'angelic' or anything. I felt like I always did. Like Keira.

"Sean..." I said, trying to stay calm. I mean, I *knew* he was an angel... and had all kinds of angel-y abilities and stuff. I also knew he was totally batshit crazy.

Crazy about you, yeah.

"Would you stop that?" I swatted him.

Nope.

"Arrrgh!"

Keira...

"Just *talk* to me, Sean. Not in my head, in my ears." I was feeling more and more afraid of him and needed at least that bit of space.

"It's easier to explain the other way," he said.

"Not for me!"

His lips pursed. "Okay, maybe you have a point..." He held my shoulders. "From the moment time itself began, we were meant for one another. Billions of years ago, in this realm's measurement, we held one another and watched as this universe was born in the Big Bang."

His smile became winsome. "We danced among the atoms as they were created, sat back and..." He reached down and took my hand. "In the same way lovers here sit on a beach and watch sunsets, we watched galaxies form. In wonder and joy, together we crossed the spans of space and time, watching all of it... *all of it* unfold!" He shook his head slowly. "It's been a glorious and blessed existence we've shared, my love."

"But... how come I don't remember?"

"Because you didn't want to."

"Huh?"

"When you decided that you wanted to join this race... meld with them, you decided at that time that you didn't want to know of your angelic nature. You wanted to experience all the moments here fully. So you had..." He shrugged. "We called them 'the scales on your eyes' when we talked about it. So you would stay blind to all else but what a human feels and is."

"Scales."

"Yeah."

"Sounds gross."

"Hey! It's your term not mine!" he said with a laugh. "*I* wanted to use a different term! But noooo! You insisted on calling them 'scales'!"

"Really."

"Mmm-hmmm." He stepped back, almost daring me to ask.

So I did. "Okay, what did you want to call this... handicap you say I have?"

"Blinders."

"Like on a horse?" I shook my head. "Scales sounds better than that!"

"See! That's what you said twenty-four years ago!"

I couldn't believe I was having this ridiculous conversation. "Okay then... what exactly was the agreement or whatever?"

He looked at me sideways. "Whaddya mean?"

"Why are you telling me this now if I was supposed to go through my life as a human? Why didn't you tell me sooner?"

He shrugged. "Because Gwen's having a baby, and you need to continue the work." He tilted his head at me. "And you *can't* do it alone."

I shrugged. "I'll find a replacement."

"For *Gwen*? Just like that?" He snickered. "I can't wait to tell her you said that!"

"Don't you dare!"

"What are you gonna do? Take an ad out on Craig's List?"

"Well, what the hell are you saying?"

"I think you met Gwen because that was meant to be. I joined the human race, her family, because of Pamela's proximity, and I suspected that you might—might—be called upon to take her place." He nodded slowly. "And I think things are unfolding as they should." He held up his hand. "No—I have *faith* that this is the way it's supposed to be."

"Faith."

"Yeah."

I sighed. Faith. "What if you're wrong? There's a thing called misplaced faith, you know."

He nodded. "That's a risk I'm willing to take. I'd rather be wrong about this than let you go through the rest of your life alone. As long as you had Gwen and Roy beside you, I knew you would be okay. But that's gonna change now…"

He was right about that. I never thought of Gwen and Roy building a life just for themselves. Creating *their* family. What a fool I had been. A selfish, self-centered idiot.

Not an idiot, darling…

I raised my head. *I don't agree.*

He smiled. *Like all living beings, you've done the best you can.*

I smiled. *Thank you.*

Do you love me?

I nodded. *From the moment I saw you…*

He barked a laugh. "That was a *looong* time ago!" He looked into my eyes. His own were swimming in colors and lights. *Do you trust me?*

I nodded. *Yes.*

Close your eyes.

I closed them and felt his hands on my face. His fingers splayed across the sides of my head, and with a gentle pressure, he stroked my eyelids. Back and forth, the pads of his thumbs caressed them. I felt a little granular rubbing, like when you rub sleep dust out of your eyes when you wake up. But different

Very, very different.

He took his hands away.

Open your eyes.

The END

Author's Note

Keira's tale is now complete. Typing 'The End' to this series was the most bittersweet experience I've ever had as a writer. I will miss her and all the others. For almost two years she's been part of my life, surprising me as I wrote her story. It's time for me to say goodbye to her and wish her well.

I truly hope you enjoyed this tale. I'm deeply grateful for you to read this book. Writers work in isolation, then send their work out into the world, holding their breath. I can honestly say I did the best I could, and hope you enjoyed reading as much as I did crafting this series.

All the best to you and yours,

Shelley Dorey

ABOUT THE AUTHOR

Michelle Dorey, writing as 'Shelley Dorey' is the author of more than twenty spine-chilling novels featuring ghosts, haunted houses and the supernatural. She has been on the Amazon best seller list many times throughout her career.

A voracious reader of the masters like Stephen King and Dean Koontz, she decided to try her hand at writing after going on a Ghost Walk in the enigmatic city of Kingston, Ontario, Canada where she lives. Her first book, Crawley House was inspired by a true tale of a family's nightmare, living in a home owned by Queen's University.

"Expect the supernatural when the bedrock of a city is limestone. Throw in the fact it is bordered on three sides by the mighty St. Lawrence River, The Rideau River and Lake Ontario and you are in for some thrills and chills of the paranormal variety--which of course is my cup of tea."

Does she love Kingston? You bet! Her husband Jim, a transplanted native New Yorker born and raised in the Bronx, agrees. Michelle and Jim like nothing better than spoiling their two pugs with treats and long walks in their neighborhood. Funny, but the slightly neurotic dogs always refuse to go for a stroll in the cemetery nearby.

OTHER WORKS

All of Michelle Dorey and Shelley Dorey books are
exclusively available on Amazon

Women's Paranormal Fantasy By Shelley Dorey

The Mystical Veil Series
Hex After 40 Series
Celtic Knot Series

Ghosts And Hauntings By Michelle Dorey

The Hauntings Of Kingston Series
The Haunted Ones Series
The Haunted Cabin